Eliminate the Impossible

An examination of the world of Sherlock Holmes on page and screen

Alistair Duncan

Paperback ISBN 9781904312314
Published in the UK by MX Publishing
10 Kingfisher Close, Stanstead Abbotts, Hertfordshire, SG12 8LQ

This book is dedicated to my wife Kate and parents, Margaret and Barrie. Thanks for all your support, assistance and patience.

Contents

Acknowledgements

My thanks go first and foremost to my wife Kate who has suffered constant talk about Sherlock Holmes ever since I made the decision to write this book. I have put her through multiple versions of the various films and dragged her around various sites including the Sherlock Holmes pub and museum. She now sits in a lounge that is occupied by a not inconsiderable amount of ornaments and prints all dedicated to the Great Detective. Despite all this she remained supportive and encouraged me whenever I started to flag.

Many thanks also go to Sir Arthur Conan Doyle without whom the world would not have Sherlock Holmes. In addition my thanks go to W.S. Baring-Gould, D. Martin Dakin, T.S. Blakeney and other authors of works examining the stories. Without their considerable efforts I would have had little to argue with and I would have remained in the dark about some of the more obscure inconsistencies in the stories. Other useful sources will be acknowledged it situ as well as in the bibliography.

Due to copyright issues the only images displayed in this book are those now in the public domain.

About the author

Alistair Duncan is an I.T. Consultant who has been a fan of Sherlock Holmes since the 1980s. Already the owner of an impressive collection of books, films and other memorabilia, he has finally decided to add to the library of books on all things Sherlockian. He lives with his wife in South London.

Introduction

Sherlock Holmes is one of the most recognisable and well known characters in literature. The image of him and Watson travelling along fog covered Victorian streets in search of clues is one that most people can easily conjure.

Like many people I gained my first glimpse into this world through television. I dimly remember, as a boy of less than ten years old, seeing the Basil Rathbone series of films for the first time. Rathbone *was* Sherlock Holmes for me for many years until I eventually started to see other adaptations. Despite this, for a long time afterwards, if I read one of the stories Rathbone was the Holmes of my imagination.

Although I have long since discovered the inaccuracies of these films they were still responsible for getting me engrossed in arguably the best known series of detective stories to date. Since that first introduction I have watched many television adaptations and read all of the original stories along with a number of pastiches by other authors. My interest has naturally extended to other crime authors but none of them for me generates the same magical imagery as the work of Sir Arthur Conan Doyle.

So many books have been written on the subject of Holmes, Watson and Conan Doyle himself that you may wonder why I am adding yet another. I am well aware from my research that many of the anomalies in the stories and films that I will later refer to have been covered to some degree in other works. I have tried as much as possible to bring a fresh perspective to some of these puzzles. Where I have been unable to contribute anything new I have attempted to weigh the pros and cons of the opinions expressed in the hope of allowing the reader to come to their own informed conclusions.

This book was originally conceived as an introduction to the canon for those that had not given the world of Holmes more than a cursory glance. However as I wrote more and delved more deeply into some of the issues I became aware that I had created a work that to some extent would appeal to people who are long-standing fans as well as novice Sherlockians. However, I can state with absolute certainty that this book is not for you if you have not read at least some of the original stories.

My last word to the reader concerns the title of this book. As any author knows, choosing a title is one of the hardest aspects of writing a book. With a book about Sherlock Holmes it is even more so. With so many books out there, all the most obvious titles have been taken. I was lucky to find a title that most Holmes fans will recognise and yet had not been used.

However please note that it is purely a title and not a mission statement. I am not offering any definitive solutions to any of the puzzles that have been faced by generations of Sherlockian scholars. I am simply offering my own viewpoint.

Alistair Duncan - London, 2008

Part One - Holmes on the page

The beginning

Sherlock Holmes was by no means the first fictional detective but he is arguably the most famous. Created by Sir Arthur Conan Doyle (1859 – 1930), he first appeared on the written page when *A Study in Scarlet* was published in *Beeton's Christmas Annual* in 1887. Conan Doyle is known to have based the character on his university professor and mentor Dr Joseph Bell.

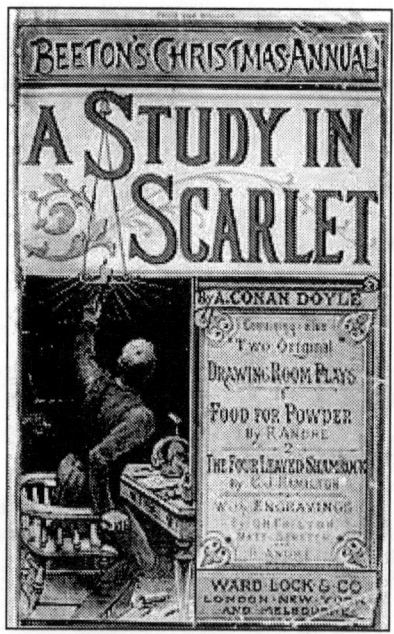

The Cover of Beeton's Christmas Annual 1887

Bell (1837 – 1911) was a lecturer at the medical school of the University of Edinburgh. He met Conan Doyle in 1877 and appointed him as his clerk in the Edinburgh Royal Infirmary.

During his lectures Bell made a point of emphasising the importance of observation when making a diagnosis. He later extended his talents into the world of crime and such was his success that it resulted in him being consulted by Scotland Yard in connection with the murders carried out by Jack the Ripper.

Dr Joseph Bell

Conan Doyle's medical career did not progress as fast as he had hoped and he increasingly used his time for writing. Inspired by Bell, he created Sherlock Holmes and ultimately captured the public's imagination.

The decision to make Holmes an amateur detective, who regularly outsmarted the official police, may well have arisen from the fact that the police of the time were not seen as particularly effective or popular. In some sections of society they were positively loathed. On 13th November 1887, a little over a month prior to the publication of *A Study in Scarlet*, the riot in Trafalgar Square known as Bloody Sunday had taken place. Police and troops, in an effort to quell the riot, had attacked the demonstrators, in many cases hurting women and children. Hundreds were treated in hospital and some demonstrators died. The media of the day, which was starting to become more like the mass media that we are used to, seized on the events of Bloody Sunday and reported them widely. The rapid expansion of the media was due in no small part to the 1870 Elementary Education Act which had led to an increasing number of the population being literate and therefore there was a much greater market for literature of all kinds.

Public confidence in the police fell even further during the Ripper murders of late 1888 when the killer seemed able to murder at will in defiance of all attempts by the police to capture him. Consequently a series of stories in which the main character repeatedly showed up the official force were bound to appeal to the public at large.

There were other advantages to having Holmes as an amateur. From Conan Doyle's perspective having Holmes independent meant that he could have him break the law in order to further his cases. This would have been a far more far fetched idea had Holmes been an official police inspector. Stories such as *The Bruce-Partington Plans* and *Charles Augustus Milverton,* where vital evidence is gained by Holmes through burglary, would not have been quite so feasible. It is also possible to argue that Conan Doyle made Holmes independent as a further homage to Bell who was himself a consultant to the official police.

For Bell the association was a two edged thing. As soon as he was publicly revealed as the 'real' Sherlock Holmes he was besieged by further requests for help in criminal cases. Bell was a man who disliked publicity and to be constantly questioned about Holmes must have been an unwelcome distraction from his work. He was later to be quoted as saying 'I am haunted by my double, Sherlock Holmes'. Despite all this he is alleged to have sent Conan Doyle ideas for stories although it is not known whether they were ever used. We can infer that they probably were not as Conan Doyle was known to refuse any form of collaboration. In 1911 the author Arthur Whitaker sent a Holmes story to Conan Doyle entitled *The Adventure of the Sheffield Banker* and suggested that they collaborate. Conan Doyle refused but ended up purchasing the manuscript in order that he could later choose to use the idea. Ultimately he did not and it was published, with Whitaker credited as author, in a collection of Holmes pastiches entitled *The Further Adventures of Sherlock Holmes*.

Such is the enduring popularity of Holmes that many authors have written their own Holmes stories in the wake of Conan Doyle's death. In fact there are now far more of these in existence than the original sixty stories. However, these pastiches are but one aspect of the huge industry that has sprung from the creation of this most famous of detectives. It is doubtful that Conan Doyle really had any conception of how his character, which he himself looked upon as unimportant, would take the world by storm.

Sherlock Holmes's influence on crime fiction

The detective novel has, at its most basic level, two forms. The chief protagonist is either an amateur detective who operates outside the official law enforcement system or he (or she) is a member of the official force.

When the detective is unofficial the author usually ensures their importance to the story by making the official police less than adequate if not downright incompetent thus forcing them to constantly turn to the unofficial detective for help and advice. The Sherlock Holmes stories took this concept to great heights with the likes of Inspector Lestrade, who was tenacious but lacking in intelligence. As we have already explored in the previous chapter, a possible reason for this portrayal of Scotland Yard was the low public confidence in the police of the time. The trend for an inadequate police force was continued by later authors such as Agatha Christie whose two principal characters, Hercule Poirot and Miss Marple, spent much time offering titbits of information to the official force while pursuing their own enquiries.

One of the features of the detective novel that Conan Doyle made comprehensive use of was the side-kick. All fictional detectives need some mechanism for explaining their reasoning to the reader. The side-kick or assistant is the most common form of this as he or she can ask all the questions that the reader would dearly like to ask the detective themselves. For Sherlock Holmes, Watson largely, but not exclusively, served this purpose. Christie's Poirot, on the other hand, often operated as a lone agent. Therefore, in the absence of a regular assistant, he often needed the official police force as his vehicle for explaining his reasoning.

Where there is an assistant the author has the dilemma of how intelligent to make him or her. Poirot's occasional side-kick, Captain Hastings, is generally accepted to be rather slow and it is this slowness that allows Christie the opportunity to enlighten both Hastings and the reader as to Poirot's reasoning. As Sherlock Holmes's friend and assistant, Dr Watson is far from unintelligent. It is a sad fact that his character is often portrayed in film and television as slow if not a downright idiot. The most famous of these portrayals was given by Nigel Bruce alongside Basil Rathbone's Holmes. Bruce's portrayal did a disservice to the character of Holmes as well as that of Watson and the effects were felt for many years afterwards.

It is true that Watson does not have the deductive powers of Holmes (it would lessen Holmes's magnificence if he did) and is thus often used as a vehicle to explain Holmes's thoughts to the reader. However, it is also frequently the case that Holmes talks to Watson about the incompetence of the police and how much he has had to help them in a given investigation. In this way Watson is more of a sympathetic ear for Holmes's outbursts of frustration rather than someone always seeking guidance. Therefore it is possible to regard Watson occasionally as a secondary vehicle for explanations occurring rather than the primary cause of them.

In addition to the assistant, literary detectives often have a 'family' of minor characters that appear irregularly in their stories. In the case of the Sherlock Holmes stories, such characters as Inspector Lestrade, Mrs Hudson, the Baker Street Irregulars and Mycroft Holmes all serve to create a sense of a world that contains more characters that just the detective, assistant, victim, villain and henchmen. Christie made use of this same concept in her Poirot stories with the characters of Chief Inspector Japp and Miss Lemon. These characters share one thing in common with the principal assistant in that they are often used by the detective to do their leg-work for them.

This tendency increases in those stories where the detective is aged (as with Miss Marple) or considers themselves above too much manual work (Poirot).

All the aspects of the detective story that have been outlined have continued over the years and are seen in stories where the detective is official as well as unofficial. The formula clearly works and no author has entirely deserted it.

The other significant feature of the Sherlock Holmes stories and others set in similar periods is the reliance on traditional or non-forensic methods of crime detection. An unavoidable aspect of modern crime stories is their heavy reliance on forensic science to solve the crime. These stories tend to be less about the crime being worked out by the detective and more about it being solved by someone in a white coat in a laboratory. Modern television dramas such as the BBC's *Waking the Dead* and *Silent Witness* follow this approach.

Back in the late nineteenth century forensic science was in its infancy. In 1887, at the time of the publication of *A Study in Scarlet*, the adoption of fingerprinting by Scotland Yard was fourteen years away. In the same story Holmes is portrayed as something of a pioneer in early forensics. Watson's former colleague Stamford informs him that Holmes had been known to beat corpses with sticks to determine how long bruises could be produced after death. On the occasion of their first meeting Holmes is triumphant at producing a chemical test for ascertaining whether or not a stain is blood (although we hear no more of it afterwards). We also learn that one of Holmes's sidelines is the composition of monographs on various subjects useful in crime detection. During the course of the stories he refers to his works on cigar and cigarette ash, document aging and the tracing of footprints.

Despite the use of these early forensic techniques, the Holmes stories still largely require the crime to be solved by deduction and a lot of physical effort. This allows us to visit many locations with the characters in order that clues can be collected and witnesses interviewed. Through this we get a better sense of the world in which the characters live and the different attitudes and morals of the time.

The appearance and character of Sherlock Holmes

The iconic appearance of Sherlock Holmes is that of the hawk nosed man in the deerstalker hat and Inverness cape; smoking a curved pipe and holding a magnifying glass. The enduring nature of this image is largely down to Basil Rathbone's portrayal of the character although the deerstalker hat was actually depicted in illustrations that accompanied some of the original stories. *The Boscombe Valley Mystery* and *The Adventure of Silver Blaze* contain illustrations in which Holmes is wearing the deerstalker (but not the Inverness cape). The curved calabash pipe was added to the image by the actor William Gillette who played Sherlock Holmes on stage in the late nineteenth and early twentieth centuries. This is one of the screen images that have overtaken reality as the kind of pipe Holmes was shown using in the illustrations was more akin to the type known as the churchwarden.

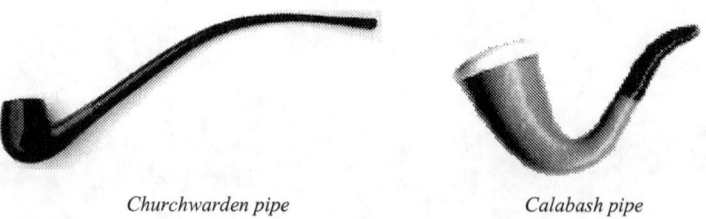

Churchwarden pipe   *Calabash pipe*

The man responsible for the image of Sherlock Holmes is the principal illustrator of the stories - Sidney Paget (1860-1908). It is entirely down to chance that Paget got the commission as the *Strand* Magazine had intended to employ his younger brother

Walter who was the more famous illustrator. A letter addressed to 'Mr Paget' fell into Sidney's hands and the rest is history.

Sidney Paget

It is generally accepted that the Holmes Paget created was based on his brother but in the 1912 edition of the *Dictionary of National Biography,* published by Smith, Elder and Co. it was stated:

> The assertion that the artist's brother Walter, or any other person, served as model for the portrait of Sherlock Holmes is incorrect.

The statement seems strange as, when you look at a picture of Walter Paget alongside an illustration of Holmes, you cannot help but remark on the similarity.

Walter Paget

Sherlock Holmes

Regardless of the original inspiration, Paget's visualisation of the character is so firmly established that the majority of actors who have portrayed Holmes on stage and screen have adhered to his vision. The same has applied to illustrators who have depicted Holmes in stories since Paget's death.

Moving onto his character, what are the words commonly associated with Sherlock Holmes? Most people when asked this come up with 'drug-addict', 'robot' and 'misogynist'. A few, usually those with little real interest or knowledge, will say 'homosexual'.

To deal with the last first, the idea that Holmes and Watson were homosexual is almost entirely based on the facts that Holmes was known to distrust women, that he and Watson shared rooms and had, what Watson himself described as, an intimate relationship. People who take the time to study the stories will find that Watson marries twice during the course of the various cases. Therefore, unless you pursue the idea that he is bisexual, the homosexual relationship theory falls apart. As for the 'intimate' relationship, it simply means that they worked hand in glove and were privy to the workings of each others minds - nothing more.

Turning to Holmes it is quite clear that he is very much a confirmed bachelor. The idea is one that people find strange nowadays but it was very common right up to the mid twentieth century. There are many people even today who live for their work at the expense of any kind of domestic life. It is simply the case that Holmes is such a person. Far from being homosexual it is more apt to describe Holmes as asexual as he clearly has no interest in any kind of romantic relationship.

The idea that Holmes lacks emotion and is more akin to a robot than a human being is, to a certain extent, backed up by the stories themselves. However, when Watson refers to Holmes as an automaton in *The Sign of Four* he is purely referring to Holmes's lack of appreciation of his client's beauty. He is not suggesting that Holmes is emotionless all of the time.

It is true that Holmes regards emotion as an obstacle to true logic but at the same time he is susceptible to very human feelings. When Watson first meets him Holmes is ecstatic about the blood test that he has just invented and whenever he is hot on the trail he is excited and full of energy. These are hardly the characteristics of a totally cold logician. When Watson is shot in *The Adventure of the Three Garridebs* Holmes shows his darker side.

'By the Lord, it is as well for you. If you had killed
Watson, you would not have got out of this room alive.
Now, sir, what have you to say for yourself?'

Unquestionably, Holmes's most well known vice is his drug
use. Cocaine is his personal favourite as described in the final
lines of *The Sign of Four*.

'"For me," said Sherlock Holmes, "there still remains the
cocaine-bottle." And he stretched his long white hand up
for it.'

At the beginning of the story Watson remarks on how he has
seen Holmes take drugs three times a day for the previous three
months. However people who think that Holmes continually
indulged in drug use could not be more wrong. For him cocaine
was simply a substitute for work and a means to avoid the
negative effects of boredom. In response to Watson's challenge
on the subject, Holmes suggested that he was able to stop and
start at will.

'My mind,' he said, 'rebels at stagnation. Give me problems,
give me work, give me the most abstruse cryptogram, or the
most intricate analysis, and I am in my own proper
atmosphere. I can dispense then with artificial stimulants.'

The clear suggestion here is that while Holmes is in constant
need of mental stimulation he is able to change how he
achieves it. In a way, work for him is a drug in itself. No doubt
modern drug addiction experts would question whether or not
this occasional drug use is really possible.

Some film adaptations of the Holmes stories have grossly
exaggerated his drug use. A good example of this can be found
in the BBC version of *The Hound of the Baskervilles* (2002)
starring Richard Roxburgh and Ian Hart. This film had Holmes,

played by Roxburgh, injecting himself just after the commencement of the case. This is completely against the known character of Holmes as he would have had no need of such a stimulant when he had just been given data to analyse. This same adaptation also had Holmes injecting himself in a railway station toilet at the height of the story just before he and Watson attempted to capture the hound. This depiction of Holmes's drug use was clearly an attempt to make him seem more in keeping with twenty-first century perceptions. The tendency to modernise the stories is something we shall return to.

Throughout the stories we see that Holmes is a man of extremes capable of amazing levels of activity and equal levels of lethargy. The former is on display whenever the chase is on and the latter whenever he is without a case or at a point in a case where he is waiting on others before he can act. Whilst in these lethargic moods he often begs to be left alone while he smokes or plays the violin. Watson is the loser on these occasions as Holmes often monopolises the use of their sitting room and he has to amuse himself elsewhere until Holmes feels sociable again. Some people have suggested that this indicates that Holmes may have been a manic depressive but this is not a view that the present author subscribes to.

As stated earlier, Holmes is something of a pioneer in the use of forensic science. During the course of his adventures he displays knowledge of such techniques as the identification and tracking of footprints and the identification of different types of cigars and cigarettes from their ash. In *Silver Blaze* Holmes is able to track the eponymous horse's movements across the ground outside of its stable and work out that a man escorted it away from the area. In *The Adventure of the Resident Patient*, Holmes is able to identify the number of involved parties by the types of ash and footprints that they leave at the murder scene. There are many similar examples throughout the canon, all of which illustrate that, as a character, Holmes was far in advance of his time.

Now we must turn our attention to the often voiced accusation of misogyny. Holmes's indifferent attitude towards women is frequently shown in the stories. There have been many different explanations put forward for this. In *The Adventure of the Second Stain,* Holmes says the following about them.

> 'Their most trivial action may mean volumes, or their most extraordinary conduct may depend upon a hairpin or curling tongs.'

This does indeed suggest a low opinion of women in general but Holmes does make the odd exception. Irene Adler from *A Scandal in Bohemia* is the most notable of these. Despite being beaten by her he leaps to her defence when she is insulted by his client, the King of Bohemia.

> 'What a woman -- oh, what a woman!' cried the King of Bohemia, when we had all three read this epistle. 'Did I not tell you how quick and resolute she was? Would she not have made an admirable queen? Is it not a pity that she was not on my level?'

> 'From what I have seen of the lady she seems indeed to be on a very different level to your Majesty,' said Holmes coldly.

In *The Sign of Four*, Holmes says of Mary Morstan.

> 'You are certainly a model client. You have the correct intuition.'

What many people conveniently overlook is the fact, often remarked upon by Watson, that Holmes is extremely courteous in his dealings with women, even more so if they are his clients. It is quite often the case that he treats them more civilly than male clients. His admiration for Irene Adler, which is genuine rather than grudging, clearly shows that he is far from being a misogynist. Being occasionally dismissive of women is very far from actively disliking them.

Despite being a servant of the law, Holmes is not a man who is afraid to break it in order to further his case. During the course of the stories he burgles and withholds evidence from the police without as much as a glimmer of conscience. As discussed earlier, it is quite probable that one of the main reasons for making Holmes an amateur detective was the option to have him break the law in ways such as these.

Holmes is also shown to be an incomparable actor willing to adopt disguises in order to achieve his end. In *A Scandal in Bohemia* he dresses as both a groom and a clergyman in order to find out the information that he needs. He repeats the clergyman, but with an Italian slant, in order to elude Professor Moriarty in *The Final Problem.* In other stories he becomes an opium addict, a bookseller, a sailor and a plumber.

Finally he is a great lover of music and, as Watson remarks, 'Plays the violin well'. In short he is a fascinating and well-rounded character which is why it is perhaps understandable that many people still believe today that he did once exist (or still does exist) for real.

"ALL AFTERNOON HE SAT IN THE STALLS."

Sherlock Holmes in The Red-Headed League

Heroes and Villains

Throughout the Sherlock Holmes stories there are characters that have made a mark on the series. In some cases these characters have made their mark by means of regular appearances; in others, the characters have become memorable despite minimal appearances or perhaps a single appearance. In this chapter we will look at some of these characters and provide a little information about them. Plot details exist here as an inevitable consequence of the descriptions.

Name: Doctor John H. Watson
First Appeared in: A Study in Scarlet

Where else could we start but with Doctor John H. Watson, Holmes's trustworthy friend and chronicler. Watson is the definitive side-kick. With him, as in so many other areas of crime fiction, Conan Doyle laid the ground rules that have been followed pretty much ever since.

Watson is an ex-army surgeon who, after qualifying in 1878, went out to fight in the second Afghan war which ran from 1843 – 1880. During the battle of Maiwand (1880) he received a serious injury (or injuries) and, while in hospital, fell ill with enteric fever. Invalided out of the army due to the permanent damage caused by this and his earlier injuries, he found himself alone and friendless in London. Like anyone else alone in a big city Watson started to feel the boredom and loneliness. In addition to this he had money troubles due to the fact that he was living in a hotel and thus beyond his long-term means. It was these concerns that ultimately brought him into contact with Sherlock Holmes.

In the opening part of *A Study in Scarlet*, Watson states that he had made up his mind that he could no longer afford to live in hotels and must therefore find lodgings. It is while he is ruminating on this conclusion that he bumps into Stamford, a former hospital colleague. Over lunch he discovers that an acquaintance of Stamford's, by the name of Sherlock Holmes, is in a similar predicament to himself. A meeting is arranged at a nearby laboratory where Watson gets his first taste of Holmes's extraordinary abilities when Holmes is able to deduce his past action in Afghanistan and where he has been wounded. The two of them inspect the lodgings at 221b Baker Street the very next day and decide to move in.

Watson (left) and Holmes in
The Final Problem

Watson's war injury is one of those subject areas in which Conan Doyle causes confusion with his inconsistency. In *A Study in Scarlet* the injury is to his shoulder. However it is also referred to as a leg injury in the opening pages of *The Sign of Four*. We shall however leave the amusing theories as to where the wound is or whether Watson had more than one to other authors.

At the beginning of their association, as told in *A Study in Scarlet*, Watson draws up the infamous list of Holmes's abilities as he then saw them. This appraisal was revised as Watson gained more insight into Holmes's methods and abilities but the list itself shows clearly how much of a mystery Holmes was to Watson.

SHERLOCK HOLMES -- his limits.
1. Knowledge of Literature. -- Nil.
2. Philosophy. -- Nil.
3. Astronomy. -- Nil.
4. Politics. -- Feeble.
5. Botany. -- Variable. Well up in belladonna, opium, and poisons generally. Knows nothing of practical gardening.
6. Geology. -- Practical, but limited. Tells at a glance different soils from each other. After walks has shown me splashes upon his trousers, and told me by their colour and consistence in what part of London he had received them.
7. Chemistry. -- Profound.
8. Anatomy. -- Accurate, but unsystematic.
9. Sensational Literature. -- Immense. He appears to know every detail of every horror perpetrated in the century.
10. Plays the violin well.
11. Is an expert singlestick player, boxer, and swordsman.
12. Has a good practical knowledge of British law.

Watson is frequently irritated by Holmes's tendency to keep things from him during a case. An example of this occurs during *The Hound of the Baskervilles* when Holmes lies to Watson and says that he cannot travel to Dartmoor with him when in fact he actually catches a later train in order to carry out investigations without Watson's knowledge. However this tendency on Holmes's part never puts their friendship or association in jeopardy as has been suggested in some screen adaptations.

One of the many criticisms levelled at Watson is that his command of the facts is somewhat shaky. Many scholars point to areas of chronology that are confused or events that they believe could not have taken place and accuse Watson of getting the facts wrong. You will see this subject dealt with several times in other sections of this book.

There are only two possible reasons why Watson is perceived to get things wrong. Either Conan Doyle intentionally wrote him as a lax chronicler or he is the recipient of Conan Doyle's own failings.

For those who believe the errors are Watson's rather than Conan Doyle's, it needs to be understood that making Watson a bad chronicler makes no sense. At the beginning of *The Sign of Four* Holmes remarks to Watson that he has looked at his account of *A Study in Scarlet* and is not pleased with the result. This displeasure is not about the facts of the case but what he perceives as Watson's attempts to make them more colourful. He makes a similar remark in *The Abbey Grange*. However the point needs to be driven home that these are not complaints about Watson's accuracy. A man such as Holmes who required that everything should be seen as it is would not have tolerated inaccuracies in the accounts of his cases.

Therefore it becomes reasonable to assume that the only reasons for perceived inaccuracies are either that they were genuine mistakes by Conan Doyle or that they were deliberate mistakes he had Watson make for the purposes of client confidentiality.

Another interesting thing about Watson is his changeable attitude towards the law. Holmes requests his assistance getting into the houses of opponents on three occasions. The first occasion occurs in *A Scandal in Bohemia* when Holmes involves Watson in his plan to get into Irene Adler's house. On this occasion Watson is only too pleased to oblige. He is similarly agreeable when Holmes seeks his participation in breaking into the home of Charles Augustus Milverton in the story of the same name. On this occasion Watson is very nearly caught. The last occasion occurs in *The Bruce-Partington Plans*. However, this time, Watson is squeamish, at first expressing his unhappiness before finally agreeing to help. This will be examined further later on.

However Watson's principal strength as far as Holmes is concerned is his ability to stimulate his own thought processes. On many occasions a remark from Watson has initiated a train of thought for Holmes which has enabled him to make a breakthrough in a case. We shall look at Watson's involvement with Holmes in greater depth during the course of this book.

Name: Mrs Hudson
First Appeared in: The Sign of Four

Mrs Hudson is a character that every Sherlock Holmes fan is aware of and yet she barely features in the stories. So little does she feature that Sidney Paget did not even depict her in any of his illustrations. It seems remarkable that a character so central to the day-to-day running of Holmes and Watson's household is so poorly served by the stories. The fact that she is Scottish is mentioned in *The Naval Treaty* but beyond this and her name little is known.

Mrs Hudson is first mentioned by name in *The Sign of Four* when Holmes asks her to show up his prospective client Mary Morstan. Her most pivotal role in the canon is when she assists with the capture of Colonel Sebastian Moran in *The Empty House* by moving a bust of Holmes in the sitting room of 221b in order that Moran should believe him to be at home and possible to assassinate.

It is an unavoidable and welcome fact that the illustrations by Sidney Paget have to a greater or lesser extent influenced the portrayal of the various characters on screen. With Mrs Hudson filmmakers have had free reign due to the absence of such illustrations. Hence the public's perception of Mrs Hudson is entirely driven by film portrayals and the imagination. For the former we can assume that the most influential appearances are those given by Mary Gordon alongside Basil Rathbone and Rosalie Williams alongside Jeremy Brett.

Both these actresses have successfully shown how tolerant Mrs Hudson had to be in order to accept a lodger such as Holmes. This is, after all, a man who frequently left his rooms in an untidy state (which on occasion even drove Watson to distraction), practised his shooting indoors and had visitors at all hours of the day and night. It is pretty safe to say that to find a live-in landlady who would accept such behaviour would be as hard in Victorian times as it certainly would be today.

Name: Inspector Lestrade
First Appeared in: A Study in Scarlet

Inspector Lestrade is considered by Holmes to be, along with Inspector Gregson, the 'pick of a bad lot'. However this is not a significant compliment as while he is complimentary about his tenacity and energy he is highly dismissive of Lestrade's deductive abilities. Consequently, Holmes tends to avoid involving Lestrade, or any official agent, unless he needs the power afforded by their official status.

One of the most curious things about Lestrade is his willingness to take the credit for cases solved by Holmes. Holmes's apparent dislike of publicity is usually cited as the motivating factor in the decision to hand the credit to Scotland Yard and Lestrade is all too happy to take it.

*Inspector Lestrade (left) in The Adventure of the
Cardboard Box*

The problem with this, for Lestrade, is that he lays himself open to eventual exposure by Watson's accounts. For an especially good example we need only to look at *The Adventure of the Empty House*. At the end of this story Holmes, in his desire to avoid publicity, hands the entire credit for the capture of the murderer of Ronald Adair to Lestrade. The resolution of such a murder would have made it into the national and possibly international press and Lestrade presumably would have been feted as a highly able detective. We can only imagine the consequences of Watson's true account of events subsequently appearing and showing that Lestrade's involvement was minimal. We can be reasonably certain that if Lestrade did not lose his job he would certainly be less inclined to associate himself with Holmes in the future knowing that his true involvement and mistakes would be subsequently presented to the public by Watson.

The fact that Lestrade is the official who makes the most appearances in the stories shows that he clearly has no problem being associated with Holmes despite being exposed to ridicule and this becomes one of the biggest anomalies of the canon. The same problem naturally applies to a lesser extent to all the other official detectives who have their cases solved for them by Holmes. It is interesting that Conan Doyle did not make any attempt to deal with this issue during the course of the stories.

In the conclusion to *The Adventure of the Empty House*, Watson remarks, upon setting foot in the sitting room of 221b, that nothing had changed. He particularly remarks on Holmes's scrap-books and reference books which '…many of our fellow citizens would have been so glad to burn.' It would not be unreasonable to suggest that as much as criminals would want Holmes's papers destroyed, Scotland Yard would wish to see Watson's papers meet a similar fate.

Name: Mycroft Holmes
First Appeared in: The Greek Interpreter

Holmes's older and supposedly more intelligent brother first gets a mention in *The Adventure of the Greek Interpreter* when Holmes decides to talk to Watson about his family background. Watson is stunned to learn that Holmes has any family as prior to this disclosure he had believed him to be an only child with no living relatives. Holmes takes Watson to meet his brother during the same story in order that they can meet Mr Melas whose story is the basis of the case. They meet at the Diogenes club which was co-founded by Mycroft for men who have no interest in conversation with their fellows. Holmes remarks to Watson:

'I have myself found it a very soothing atmosphere.'

As Holmes explains to Watson, Mycroft, although superior intellectually to himself, has no energy and therefore is totally ill-equipped to be a detective and actually considers it to be more of a hobby than a proper career. His own career is in government working in a position which Holmes describes, in *The Adventure of the Bruce-Partington Plans,* as

'...unique. He has made it for himself. There has never been anything like it before, nor will be again...'

In short, Mycroft receives the conclusions from all government departments and has a brain well suited to marshalling the facts he receives. This puts him in the unique position of being able to say exactly how the actions of one government department will affect another and how the actions of other countries will affect Great Britain. Mycroft's encyclopaedic knowledge comes in useful in his second appearance during *The Adventure of the Bruce Partington Plans* when he is able to provide Holmes with the details of the various government employees involved and the details of international spies who may have been in the market for the stolen plans.

Alas, due to his intelligence, it was not possible for him to feature more regularly than he did. As with all the intelligent characters in the series he could not appear too often as that would have lessened the impact of Holmes.

Mycroft Holmes as featured in The Adventure of the Greek Interpreter (Wikipedia)

Name: Professor Moriarty
First Appeared in: The Final Problem

Here we have one of the more amusing facts about the world of Sherlock Holmes. If you ask people who Holmes's greatest enemy was they will mostly say Professor Moriarty. Yet this character who, according to Holmes, was responsible for more than half the evil in London is only mentioned in two of the stories and only meets Holmes in *The Final Problem* where Conan Doyle originally intended them to both meet their end. According to Holmes, Moriarty is a genius whose treatise on asteroids brought him great fame and a high position at one of England's smaller universities. Eventually some small, unnamed, scandal overtook him and he was forced to resign. At this point he travelled to London and turned his gifted brain to crime.

Moriarty has the distinction of having become the original super villain, powerful mentally but not physically. When Conan Doyle revealed that Holmes had survived his battle with Moriarty in *The Final Problem* it was hardly surprising as Holmes was bound to win any physical battle being the younger man and a man who had knowledge of many contact sports such as boxing and fencing.

Moriarty will be discussed further in the sections on *The Final Problem* and *The Valley of Fear.*

Moriarty as featured in the
Adventure of the Final
Problem (Wikipedia)

Name: Sir Henry Baskerville
First Appeared in: The Hound of the Baskervilles

Sir Henry Baskerville is the Canadian nephew of Sir Charles Baskerville who, at the beginning of the story, has recently died from heart failure. He arrives in London and immediately finds himself in the heart of a mystery.

There was no pressing need for the character to be Canadian (or indeed any nationality in particular) therefore it seems likely that the character was created as such for the benefit of Conan Doyle's North American fans who were some of the most vocal in the campaign for Holmes's return after the events of *The Final Problem*.

Conan Doyle was known to be especially pro-American so one has to wonder why he did not make Henry Baskerville an American. A possible explanation for this could concern the Baronetcy that he inherited. It is plausible that Conan Doyle feared that having an American accept a British title would cause offence to his American readers so he made Sir Henry Canadian to get over this potential problem and at the same time make him a member of the same continent.

One of the most bizarre things about the many screen adaptations of *The Hound of the Baskervilles* is the various nationalities that are attributed to Sir Henry. Conan Doyle is decidedly unambiguous about his nationality, clearly stating that he was a farmer in Canada when he heard of his inheritance. Whilst some adaptations have kept to the story, others have insisted upon changing it even though it has little or no bearing on the plot. Over the years we have had Sir Henry's that were American, English and South African.

Name: Jonathan Small

First Appeared in: The Sign of Four

Jonathan Small is a strange character whose entire conduct during *The Sign of Four* is driven by his desire to do right by his companions. Throughout the entire story he acts as though he occupies the moral high ground and manages to totally ignore the fact that he has helped to bring about two murders and has scared another man to death.

Small's life in India, as told by him after his arrest, makes uncomfortable reading. At times you can almost find yourself thinking that the poor man had been dealt a very bad hand by life and perhaps even deserved the good life that the Agra treasure would have brought him.

Soon after arriving in India, and not even twenty years old, he has his leg bitten off by a crocodile. Following this he is able to secure work on a plantation but a short while after beginning his new duties he gets caught up in the Sepoy Rebellion and flees to fort of Agra where he is put in charge of one of the many doors into the fortress. He is assisted in his duties by two Sikh soldiers who soon tempt him with a share of the treasure of a local Rajah who is sending some of his wealth to Agra. It is Small's silence and greed that enable his companions to kill the treasure's courier.

Eventually they are discovered and sentenced to imprisonment. Small's conversations with Major Sholto and Captain Morstan, who run the prison, eventually lead to them being invited to share the treasure in exchange for freedom. Sholto betrays them all and takes the treasure to England. Small then dedicates his life to Sholto's destruction and the recovery of the treasure.

Disconcertingly, the murder of the Rajah's courier is almost ignored during Small's confession. We can only hope that this is because Small had already served his punishment for that crime. The only other possibility would be that the courier's life was considered less important than that of Captain Morstan, Major Sholto and Bartholomew Sholto. This is extremely unlikely and is only mentioned as a possibility. As D. Martin Dakin points out, all those present at Small's confession fail to grasp the fact that the only person with any moral entitlement to the Agra treasure is the Rajah from whom it was taken and his descendents. The idea that Small, his companions or Mary Morstan are in any way entitled to the treasure on any grounds would have had no legal standing whatsoever.

Name: Irene Adler (The Woman)
First Appeared in: A Scandal in Bohemia

Irene Adler holds the unique position of being the only person to have outwitted Holmes and lived. The reader should be reminded that the murderers in *The Adventure of the Resident Patient* also eluded Holmes although it was assumed they died when the ship they were thought to be on sank.

She is described as an opera singer, born in America who had met the King of Bohemia in Warsaw. During their brief liaison she had procured a photograph of herself with the King that she was subsequently to threaten him with in the story.

Holmes during his initial interview with the King is very much on his side and ready to help. You could take the view that he looked forward to the prospect of outwitting a woman who he was already aware was formidable from the details told to him by the King. What is beyond doubt is that his opinions changed during the course of the story ending with his attitude towards the King becoming decidedly confrontational and his attitude to Adler becoming one of respect. It is this respect that leads to him granting her the title of *The Woman*.

Watson makes clear in the account of the case that Holmes had no romantic interest in Adler but this has not stopped other writers assuming otherwise. W.S Baring-Gould even goes as far as to suggest that during the period between his faked death and resurrection he was to conduct a romantic liaison with Adler which produced a son. This idea was explored in the film *Sherlock Holmes in New York*. Elsewhere it was even suggested that the American detective Nero Wolfe was their son.

The timeline of the stories

Conan Doyle did not write the Sherlock Holmes stories in strict chronological order. For example, *The Hound of the Baskervilles,* which he wrote following the death of Holmes in *The Final Problem*, was written in 1901 but set before the *Final Problem* which, although written in 1893, was set in 1891.

There has been considerable debate about the true chronological order of the stories and more than one book has provided a chronology along with very detailed reasons for the time line shown. The simple fact is that Conan Doyle was so prone to contradicting himself and omitting details that it is impossible to put together a chronology that everyone will agree upon. This continuing lack of agreement is largely responsible for the large number of books that have been published about the stories and their inconsistencies (which of course this is one.) It is questionable whether Conan Doyle himself had any real time line in mind, largely because he initially had no plans to go beyond the first two novels and two sets of short stories. It is also a valid point to wonder whether it really matters. Do the inconsistencies affect the quality or enjoyment of the stories? The answer for most people is probably no. However the scope for speculation that the confused chronology offers is too much to resist for most scholars.

For example, D. Martin Dakin, in his book *A Sherlock Holmes Commentary* presented the reader with a chronology that challenged some of the generally accepted dates shown in other books. In particular he presented a case for *The Hound of the Baskervilles* being set after *The Final Problem* rather than before it as is more generally accepted. There are other examples from other authors as we shall see later. To illustrate the differences we shall present here three chronologies. For each story we shall show the date from *The New Annotated Sherlock Holmes,* Dakin's equivalent date and dates found on the Internet. Where the differences are significant the reasons will be explored in the following chapter.

Adventure	Annotated	Dakin	Internet
A Study In Scarlet	1881	1881	1881
The Sign of Four	1888	1888	1887/1888
A Scandal in Bohemia	1889	1889	1888
The Red Headed League	1890	1890	1890
A Case of Identity	1889	1889	1888
The Boscombe Valley Mystery	1889	1890	1888
The Five Orange Pips	1889	1889	1887
The Man with the Twisted Lip	1889	1889	1889
The Blue Carbuncle	1889	1889	N/A
The Speckled Band	1883	1883	1883

The Engineer's Thumb	1889	1889	1889
The Noble Bachelor	1888	1888	1887
The Beryl Coronet	1886	1886	1886
The Copper Beeches	1890	1885	N/A
Silver Blaze	1888	1888	1888
The Yellow Face	1888	1886	1888
The Stockbroker's Clerk	1889	1889	N/A
The Gloria Scott	1874	1874	N/A
The Musgrave Ritual	1879	1879	N/A
The Reigate Squires	1887	1887	1887
The Crooked Man	1889	1889	N/A
The Resident Patient	1887	1881	N/A
The Greek Interpreter	1888	1884	1888
The Naval Treaty	1889	1889	1889
The Final Problem	1891	1891	1891

The Hound of the Baskervilles	1889	1900	1889
The Empty House	1894	1894	1894
The Norwood Builder	1894	1894	1894
The Dancing Men	1898	1898	1898
The Solitary Cyclist	1895	1895	1895
The Priory School	1901	1900	1901
Black Peter	1895	1895	1895
Charles Augustus Milverton	1899	1899	N/A
The Six Napoleons	1900	1900	1899
The Three Students	1895	1895	1895
The Golden Pince-Nez	1894	1894	1894
The Missing Three-Quarter	1896	1897	1896
The Abbey Grange	1897	1897	1897
The Second Stain	1894	1894	1888
The Valley of Fear	1888	1888	N/A
Wisteria Lodge	1895	1894	1892

The Cardboard Box	1888	1888	1888
The Red Circle	1902	1897	N/A
The Bruce-Partington Plans	1895	1895	1895
The Dying Detective	1890	1890	1890
The Disappearance of Lady Frances Carfax	1901	1897	N/A
The Devil's Foot	1897	1897	1897
His Last Bow	1914	1914	1914
The Illustrious Client	1902	1902	1902
The Blanched Soldier	1903	1903	1903
The Mazarin Stone	1903	1903	N/A
The Three Gables	1902	1903	N/A
The Sussex Vampire	1896	1896	N/A
The Three Garridebs	1902	1902	1902
The Problem of Thor Bridge	1901	1901	1900

The Creeping Man	1903	1903	1903
The Lion's Mane	1907	1907	1907
The Veiled Lodger	1896	1896	1896
Shoscombe Old Place	1902	1902	1902
The Retired Colourman	1899	1898	1898

The stories

Inevitably this chapter contains a few plot details which cannot be avoided. However it is strongly suggested that the reader should study each story before reading its entry within these pages. The reader that chooses not to do so may find themselves confused by the points raised herein.

Where we state the date the story is set in we are using the chronology listed in *The New Annotated Sherlock Holmes*. However this is done for consistency and is not a statement of personal preference. The dates given for publication, which come from the same source, refer to the Strand magazine unless, as in the case of the first two stories, it was not the publication used. In some cases the stories were published in other magazines before they appeared in the Strand but we will not concern ourselves with that here.

The main purpose of this chapter is to look at some of the problems with the stories as identified by other authors. Consequently we shall not be looking at the plots of the stories in depth. Some stories will get less attention than others. Where this is occurs it is because the story does not offer as much scope for discussion as others.

The Problem with 'Playing the game'

There is a practice amongst many Sherlockian societies that is referred to as 'playing the game'. Essentially this means that we take the position that, far from being fictional stories written by Conan Doyle, these accounts really were written by Watson (with some exceptions) and are depicting real historical events.

This is unquestionably a fertile angle to adopt. The many inconsistencies within the stories offer an almost infinite number of interpretations. It is for this reason that there are so many books on the stories that work from this position. However there are significant downsides to it as well. In an effort to make everything fit with real events, the writer is forced to account for every problem with the chronology, every wrinkle in the plot and every character that is obviously fictional.

Authors working from this position go to great lengths to account for such problems in the stories. The fact that, outside of their books, they accept that the stories are fictional is put to one side in order that they can put forward their arguments. If a character is fictional it must be a guise for a real historical figure and equally great lengths are gone to in order to determine who it could be. If a date is wrong it must be because Watson had a bad recollection of events. If Watson states something that does not fit with known history then it must be a cover up for something else or is taken as evidence of his incompetence. These deliberations can be entertaining (the present author has enjoyed reading many of them) but can lead to rather bizarre results as we shall see later. As Holmes himself might say 'How can you build on such a quicksand?'

In many cases it simply has to be accepted that the inconsistencies are the result of Conan Doyle's own errors as a writer and not those of Watson. However, in order to be even handed, we shall look at these anomalies from both perspectives wherever possible.

A Study in Scarlet

Published: December 1887
Set in: 1881
Client: Scotland Yard

Synopsis: After meeting Holmes for the first time Watson accompanies him when he is called in for advice by Scotland Yard in a case where a man has been found dead in a deserted house with a look of terror on his face and no wounds. In addition there is a pool of blood that does not appear to belong to the victim.

Notes: A large portion of this story is told in flashback. This no doubt explains why this story has rarely been adapted for the screen. To get audiences to sit through a flashback sequence of such a length would be almost impossible. This was the first Holmes story to be illustrated and the illustrations were produced by D. H. Friston. They, like the story, were not overly successful. Sidney Paget was not to come on the scene until the stories began to be published in the *Strand* in 1891.

Conan Doyle sold the rights to the story for twenty-five pounds. He had initially sought royalties but was refused. Needless to say he was less than happy with the amount but he was destined to gain a degree of vengeance for this. When the short stories became popular in the *Strand*, Ward Lock & Co, who had bought the rights from Conan Doyle, asked him to write a new preface for *A Study in Scarlet*. They were presumably eager to benefit from the favourable publicity for Sherlock Holmes. Conan Doyle refused their request.

Returning to the story itself, one of the most curious aspects of it is that it features two police inspectors of equal rank sharing command of the investigation. This is an almost unique event in the stories and one wonders how often two inspectors would have been assigned to a single investigation. We are used to seeing large teams of investigators in modern murder cases but Scotland Yard was a much smaller organisation in the late 1800s. Perhaps Conan Doyle was seeking to introduce his new audience to as many characters as he could. Another possibility is that having two official detectives on the case, each of whom was out to show up the other, gave Holmes just the environment to show them both up. We can but wonder what the police of the day thought of Conan Doyle's depiction of their abilities.

The biggest problem with this story for scholars of the 'playing the game' school is the second part entitled 'The Country of the Saints'. This is the part of the story that is told in flashback in an effort to explain what led to the crimes in London. The murderer, Jefferson Hope, dies in his cell, from an aneurism, soon after his arrest so who wrote the tale?

Dakin takes the view that Hope had been keeping an account of events ever since he had begun his quest and this seems reasonable as he hardly had the time to write it in his cell after his arrest. However the problem with this, as Dakin himself acknowledges, is that parts describe events that Hope was not directly privy to. This of course begs the question of how these conversations could be noted down. Dakin explores the idea that Watson travelled to the area in order to fill in the gaps of the narrative. However, after a brief look at the practicality of the idea, he steps back describing it as '...too fantastic to merit further attention.'

It is amusing that this part of the story, told from a third-person perspective, should cause such problems. Scholars were destined to wrestle with many similar problems with stories at the tail end of the canon. There will be more of this later.

The Sign of Four

Published: February 1890
Set in: 1888
Client: Miss Mary Morstan

Synopsis: Holmes and Watson are approached by Miss Mary Morstan about the disappearance of her father some ten years previously. She explains that every year for the past six years she has received a large pearl in the mail from an anonymous benefactor. She then adds that she has recently received a letter in which her benefactor offers to meet her and answer all her questions.

Notes: This story also contains some flashback sequences when the events that led to the discovery of the Agra treasure are revealed by Jonathan Small. However it is a small amount of the overall story and therefore does not require too much time. As a result, next to *The Hound of the Baskervilles,* this is one of the most often filmed stories. During the story we are given many insights in Holmes's opinion on women and his drug use. This story is also the first in which their landlady, Mrs Hudson, is referred to by name.

The Sign of Four contains one pivotal moment. In the early pages Watson, who is still to a certain extent sceptical about his friend's deductive powers, challenges Holmes to reconstruct the late owner of a watch that has recently come into his possession. Holmes does so and deduces that the watch had belonged to Watson's brother who after periods of prosperity and 'low water' had taken to drink and died. Watson is extremely upset at the accuracy of Holmes's deductions and suggests that he must have heard about his brother's circumstances earlier. Holmes assures him that he did not and states:

> 'I assure you, however, that I never even knew that you had a brother until you handed me the watch.'

This moment is important as it really marks Watson's transition from sceptic to believer and whilst he would never cease to be amazed by Holmes's conclusions he would very rarely assume that Holmes was tricking him or cheating him. Despite the importance of this moment one author decided to ignore it in order to lend weight to his own theory about Watson's life.

Much debate has taken place on the subject of Watson and women. More specifically the debate has been focused on his marriages. It is clearly stated during the events of *The Sign of Four* that Watson and Mary Morstan become engaged at the end and their resultant marriage causes Watson to move out of Baker Street and back into medical practice. It is alleged by some that Mary is his second wife.

W.S Baring-Gould, in his book *Sherlock Holmes – A biography of the world's first consulting detective*, is an advocate of the theory that Watson met his first wife in America or, more specifically, San Francisco. This idea is not Baring-Gould's own. The suggestion was apparently made in a then unpublished play by Conan Doyle called *Angels of Darkness*. Baring-Gould suggests that in early 1883 Watson received a letter from America to state that his brother was seriously unwell. He further states that Holmes actually paid for Watson to travel to America to look after his brother. He goes on to suggest that Watson entered into medical practice whilst abroad and through this he met his first wife Constance who was his patient. Since then the play has been published and it was revealed that the name of the lady in question was Lucy

Ferrier, formerly the wife of Jefferson Hope from *A Study in Scarlet*.

Regardless of the confusion over the lady's name, we can accept that Watson could have indeed met his wife in America when running a medical practice there. However his reason for visiting in the first place could not have been to see his ailing brother. If that were the case Holmes would not be able to claim ignorance of said brother at the commencement of *The Sign of Four* which took place five years later.

Baring-Gould, as stated earlier, omits the whole exchange concerning the watch when he comes to describe *The Sign of Four*. He thus removes the need to explain the inconsistency between the story and his own version of events. There is however a plausible additional reason for the removal of the watch discussion. At the time Conan Doyle wrote *The Sign of Four* it was only Holmes's second documented case. Conan Doyle had probably given little thought to future adventures, or any kind of systematic chronology, perhaps taking the pessimistic view that as his previous story had not done very well his current one would not do well either. In this he was destined to be correct. The fame of Holmes and Conan Doyle himself would not become established until the publication of the first set of short stories in the *Strand*. Therefore, at the time of writing the story, there were no other cases apart from *A Study in Scarlet* and it therefore made sense, from the reader's perspective, for Watson to still be sceptical when it came to Holmes's deductive powers. As more stories were published Conan Doyle started to write them in a non-chronological order. As a result some of the stories that form *The Adventures of Sherlock Holmes* are actually set before the events of *The Sign of Four*. As Watson was involved in these it starts to become implausible for him to be still sceptical about Holmes's abilities come the events of *The Sign of Four*. Had Conan Doyle published a number of cases between *A Study in Scarlet* and *The Sign of Four* it is doubtful that the scene with the watch would have been written within it or, if it had, Watson would not have been so surprised at what information Holmes would be able to draw from it regardless of how upsetting such information would be.

This highlights the very different conclusions that can be drawn about the stories. If you work from the perspective of the entire published canon, certain events depicted in the stories do not make sense. If, however, you look from the perspective of what Conan Doyle had written and published at the time, events can make sense or be interpreted completely differently. We shall see other examples of this.

The Adventures of Sherlock Holmes

Contains twelve stories published 1891–1892 with original illustrations by Sidney Paget. The original Strand commission was for six but this was increased to twelve when the popularity of the stories became apparent.

A Scandal in Bohemia

Published: July 1891
Set in: 1889
Client: The King of Bohemia

Synopsis: The King of Bohemia engages Holmes and Watson to steal a photograph of him taken with a lady named Irene Adler. Miss Adler has threatened to send the photograph to the family of the King's fiancée on the day that his engagement is announced. Despite several attempts to secure it he has failed so he has come to Holmes as a last resort.

Notes: This story causes us an issue very early on. In it Watson states that it is March 1888 and the events are taking place after his marriage. However in *The Naval Treaty*, which most chronologies agree is set in 1889, Watson refers to that particular case taking place in the July after his

The King of Bohemia (left), Watson and Holmes in A Scandal in Bohemia.

marriage. This infers that Watson married in late 1888 or early 1889. This notion is further endorsed by the fact that the King of Bohemia extracts the promise from both Holmes and Watson that they will keep the events of the case secret for two years. Given that the story was published in 1891, and assuming that Conan Doyle's intention was to have us believe that Watson published the details immediately upon the expiry of the pledge, the case has to have taken place in 1889.

So why does the story say 1888? Dakin puts forward the idea that Watson simply got confused and was thinking about his wedding when he wrote 1888 or that he had bad handwriting. However why would Conan Doyle have Watson make such a mistake when it served no purpose and had no influence on the plot? Perhaps we should simply accept that the mistake is Conan Doyle's rather than Watson's.

Continuing the theme of anomalies, there is a curious reference in this story to a Mrs Turner. Said Mrs Turner is referred to as the landlady which is at odds with the previous story. There has been much discussion in other books on the possible meaning behind this reference. However all such discussion has to begin with the question – did Conan Doyle write this name by mistake? You could suggest that he had forgotten that he had already used the name of Mrs Hudson. It would not be the last time that he would contradict in one story what he had said in an earlier one. In *The New Annotated Sherlock Holmes* it is reported that in the manuscript for the story *The Empty House* the name Mrs. Turner again features but has been crossed out and replaced with Hudson. This lends some weight to the argument that it was a mistake. Another interpretation is that Mrs Turner was a stand-in while Mrs Hudson was on holiday.

Finally we must look at the King of Bohemia himself. Other authors have tried to link this character with a real life person as there was no such monarch. Baring-Gould lends his weight to the idea proposed by Edgar W. Smith, in *A Scandal in Identity,* that the King was in fact the future Edward VII. This idea does not have much to commend it. If it were the case there would have been a much longer period of secrecy imposed than two years. In fact it is doubtful whether the case would ever have been allowed to see the light of day. The King himself states that after two years the matter will be '...of no importance.' Given that such a story would have caused a great scandal for a lot longer than two years the Edward idea starts to fall apart. Predictably, after the omission of the watch episode from *The Sign of Four,* in Baring-Gould's Holmes biography the request for two years' secrecy is omitted which of course helps lend some weight to the Prince Edward theory.

Some authors would no doubt argue that Watson's account was deliberately written to make it as hard as possible to determine the true identity of the King. However this would make him absurdly inconsistent as a character. These same authors accuse Watson of being a lax chronicler who lists inaccurate dates and gets all manner of other facts wrong. Can he suddenly become the genius who can hide a member of our royal family with a fictitious name? Perhaps these same authors will next suggest that Holmes told him what to write.

Surely it is simpler (and more plausible) to accept that Conan Doyle invented the kingdom and King to avoid upsetting any existing royal houses. It would not be the first or last time that an author invented a country or monarchy. Anthony Hope in his novel *The Prisoner of Zenda* invented an entire country and monarchy so why can we not accept that Conan Doyle did the same?

The Red-Headed League

Published: August 1891
Set in: 1890
Client: Jabez Wilson

Synopsis: Jabez Wilson, a London Pawnbroker, approaches Holmes and Watson about a strange organisation called the 'Read-Headed League'.

A position within the league had come vacant and been advertised in the papers. Wilson applied for the post, after being shown the advertisement by his assistant Vincent Spaulding, and had secured the position following a brief interview with its enigmatic leader Duncan Ross. Eight weeks later the job had suddenly come to an end and the league dissolved. Wilson wants Holmes to find out why.

Notes: It was made plain in the Granada television series that this plot was masterminded by Moriarty but there is nothing to suggest this in the story. Holmes himself refers to the 'ingenious' mind of John Clay who they

Holmes and Watson meet John Clay in The Red-Headed League

capture attempting to steal gold from the City and Suburban Bank. This certainly suggests that there was no one else involved in the conception of the plan. Baring-Gould, like Granada, also suggests the involvement of Moriarty. Regrettably he does this for a number of other stories. He clearly felt the need to create a long running battle of wills between Holmes and Moriarty perhaps in order to demonstrate to the reader the abilities of Moriarty and provide a reason for Moriarty's persecution of Holmes in *The Final Problem*.

Returning to the story there is a query as to the identity of Inspector Peter Jones. Jones refers to the 'Sholto murder' and 'the Agra treasure'. From this you could infer that he is really Athelney Jones, the inspector from *The Sign of Four* and that Conan Doyle has made another mistake. However an alternative explanation is that this could genuinely be a different Jones who had simply heard about the other case from the official police records and knew of Holmes's significant involvement.

According to Baring-Gould, the events of the *Red-Headed League* take place in 1887 before the events of *The Sign of Four*. This makes it impossible for Inspector Jones (be he Peter or Athelney) to refer to the 'Sholto murder' because the events of that case would be in the future. Baring-Gould attempts to get round this by suggesting that Watson was deliberately trying to confuse the reader with inaccurate facts in his original version of the story. This kind of excuse is too often brought out as a kind of 'get out of jail free' card whenever a theory starts to fall apart.

Baring-Gould also puts forward the bizarre theory that Athelney Jones was the notorious serial killer Jack the Ripper. Aside from being a decidedly desperate attempt to merge fantasy and reality and have the Ripper murders solved by Holmes (an idea later to be used by Hollywood) it is also, from a different perspective, rather interesting and decidedly clever.

If it were true it would mean that during *The Sign of Four* Athelney Jones would already have murdered his first two victims (if you accept that there were only the five generally accepted victims of the Ripper) and the reason for the long gap (twenty-two days) between the second and third murders was that Jones was busy in the meantime working with Holmes investigating the Agra treasure.

The whole theory is instantly jeopardised if you accept the chronologies of Klinger and Dakin who place the events of *The Red-Headed League* after *The Sign of Four*. If you were to accept both this chronology and Baring-Gould's Ripper theory, Peter Jones would have to be a different policeman as Athelney Jones would hardly still be serving having been unmasked by Holmes as the Ripper. Incidentally, Dakin refers to Baring-Gould's theory and dismisses it.

A Case of Identity

Published: September 1891
Set in: 1889
Client: Miss Mary Sutherland

Synopsis: Hosmer Angel, a clerk in London, disappears just before he is due to marry. When her own family prove disinterested in locating him, his fiancée comes to Holmes for help.

Notes: The most debated aspect of this story is where Holmes agrees with the perpetrator that he has done nothing actionable. This is clearly wrong. Up until the early twentieth century, failure to honour an offer of marriage was known as 'breach of promise' and was an act pursuable in the civil courts. This was especially so if, when the offer was made, the man had no intention or way of honouring it. This civil wrong was very much a one-way thing in that it was, in practice, only possible for a man to be accused. At the time most women were dependent on their husband's income. So, if a man were to back out of a marriage, it could have disastrous financial consequences for the woman as people might assume that something amiss with her caused her would-be husband to back out of the arrangement. This would make it hard if not impossible for the lady to marry in future.

This story is generally accepted to be one of the duller of the series as Holmes solves the mystery from Baker Street and consequently there is very little of the classic Holmes style investigation that most fans are used to. In *The Greek Interpreter* Holmes states to Watson that his brother Mycroft could only be a detective 'If the art of the detective began and ended in reasoning from an arm-chair...' That being the case this was clearly more suitable for Mycroft.

Dakin expresses his surprise about Holmes's decision to withhold the truth of the case from his client Miss Sutherland. He makes the not unreasonable point that it would hardly be fair to charge his client without having delivered a result. Bearing in mind the character of Holmes it seems likely that no charge would have been made.

The Boscombe Valley Mystery

Published: October 1891
Set in: 1889
Client: Alice Turner

Synopsis: Mr Charles McCarthy, an Australian living in England, is murdered on the grounds of his estate. The prime suspect is his son James who admits to having argued with his father shortly before his death. Holmes is engaged by James's childhood friend Alice Turner, the daughter of a neighbouring Australian landowner, to prove his innocence.

The Boscombe Valley Mystery

Notes: This is the first story in which Paget depicts Holmes in the iconic Deerstalker hat. The picture is very similar to that which he drew later to illustrate *Silver Blaze*.

Dakin highlights a glaring error made by Conan Doyle, which he naturally attributes to Watson. The error in question is where Watson refers to his experience of camp life as a solider making him '...a prompt and ready traveller.' Dakin points out that Watson supposedly qualified as a doctor in 1878 and took a course before being posted to India. As he was wounded and put out of active service in 1880 at the battle of Maiwand he could only have been a serving army surgeon for a year or so at most. This hardly qualifies Watson as a seasoned campaigner.

Holmes's attitude towards John Turner raises questions. This is a man who, by his own admission, had killed people in order to amass his fortune and, subsequently, his various English properties. Holmes seems far too ready to accept Turner's suggestion that he has lived a good life since in an attempt at atonement. Turner's tirade against McCarthy as a 'devil incarnate' is rather rich coming from a multiple murderer and it is surprising that Holmes does not remark upon it. McCarthy was obviously a blackmailer but this is clearly a less serious crime than murder. However the fact that Turner is a diabetic probably has a lot to do with Holmes's attitude. The practice of injecting insulin was decades away. Therefore Turner was likely to be suffering from the long-term effects of untreatable diabetes. The limp that Holmes deduced when examining the footprints at the murder scene was almost certainly a result of Turner's condition.

The Five Orange Pips

Published: November 1891
Set in: 1889
Client: John Openshaw

Synopsis: Colonel Openshaw, a veteran of the American Confederate Army, returns to England having emigrated some years before. His nephew John Openshaw goes to live with him in his home and help run the estate. Some time after his return the colonel receives five orange pips in the mail with the letters KKK inscribed on the envelope. He reacts by taking a metal box from his private room and burning all the papers within it. He later makes a will which leaves his entire estate to his brother - John's father.

Shortly after this he is found dead apparently as a result of an accident and his brother inherits the estate. Some time after this Openshaw's father receives a letter containing five orange pips and the instruction to leave some papers on the sundial. Openshaw's father decides to ignore this and is found dead soon afterwards. Now young Openshaw has received the orange pips and, on the advice of a friend, has come to Holmes.

Notes: This is the first story in which Holmes's client is killed before the case is over. The murderers also escape Holmes despite him successfully identifying them. They are presumed lost when the ship they were travelling on sinks en route to America. Conan Doyle was to repeat this idea in *The Resident Patient*. This story is also unusual as Watson refers to the fact that his wife is on a visit to see her mother. Assuming that this is the former Mary Morstan, whom Watson married shortly after the events of *The Sign of Four,* there is an inconsistency as she herself stated at the beginning of that story that her mother was dead. This story is set only a year after the previous story so it is pretty clear that Conan Doyle made a mistake. This lends weight to the idea that naming the landlady Mrs Turner in *A Scandal in Bohemia* was also an error. In some later editions of the story an aunt is substituted for the reference to Mary's mother.

We earlier saw how W. S. Baring-Gould omitted a whole scene from *The Sign of Four* in order to avoid an inconsistency in his Holmes biography. Unfortunately we have another example with this story. Once again, Baring-Gould tries to make Professor Moriarty the mastermind behind the case. He had previously done this, as we have seen, with the *Red-Headed League*. However, in order to achieve his end on this occasion, he actually deviates from the original text. This highlights once again the significant downside of writing such books from the perspective that it is all true. A lot of the inconsistencies in the stories simply cannot be removed without changing the stories as laid down.

The change in this case is to a letter that Holmes addresses to the murderer of John Openshaw. In Conan Doyle's original text Holmes places five orange pips into an envelope and writes 'S.H. for J.O.' on the flap. The letter is then addressed to a Captain James Calhoun. Baring-Gould decides to remove the Ku Klux Klan from their involvement in the story and relegates them to the status of a blind used by Moriarty. In his version of events Moriarty is behind the murder of Openshaw and, in order to make this convincing, Baring-Gould changes the message on the flap of the envelope to 'S.H. for J.M.' thus replacing John Openshaw with James Moriarty. Then he alters the letter's destination to a mysterious address which is kept from Watson.

The burning question of course is, why go to all this trouble to integrate Moriarty into stories other than those in which Conan Doyle chose to involve him? We must never forget that Moriarty was created for one purpose, to kill Holmes. His mission was accomplished for ten years before Holmes was officially resurrected. Conan Doyle then brought Moriarty back in *The Valley of Fear,* which we will examine later. If Conan Doyle had intended him to be more of a feature he would have written him into more stories. As already suggested, the only possible reason is that Baring-Gould was trying to make sense of the interview between Holmes and Moriarty in *The Final Problem* where the latter lists the occasions where Holmes has got in his way without giving enough specifics for the reader to identify which cases he is referring to.

One final note on this story concerns Holmes's education. The issue of his university is looked at elsewhere but this story does give us a potential clue to his chosen subject. During the case Holmes and Watson discuss the latter's list of Holmes's attributes as drawn up in *A Study in Scarlet.* Watson briefly runs through the list and towards the end mentions that Holmes is, amongst other things, a 'violin-player, boxer, swordsman, lawyer, and self-poisoner by cocaine and tobacco'. So was Holmes studying law at university or is Watson's use of the term simply a way of emphasising Holmes's strong grasp of British law?

The Man with the Twisted Lip

Published: December 1891
Set in: 1889
Client: Mrs St. Clair

Synopsis: Neville St. Clair is a successful worker in the City
with a wife and young child. St Clair's wife, on a visit to
London, ends up the wrong part of town and is surprised to see
her husband looking at her from the window of a run down
house. When she spots him he screams and vanishes from view.
Worried about him she attempts to force her way into the
building but is prevented from doing so. She returns with the
police who force their way into an empty room which contains
nothing apart from local beggar Hugh Boone, some of St
Clair's clothes and a few bloodstains on the window. When the
police investigation stalls she calls in Holmes to discover what
has happened to her husband.

Hugh Boone from The Man with the Twisted Lip

Notes: The error that most authors gravitate to with this story appears very early on. The story opens at Watson's house where he lives with his new wife Mary. They receive an unexpected visit from her friend Kate Whitney who has come to beg for help in finding her opium addicted husband. Before this discussion begins Mary asks Kate whether or not she should send 'James' off to bed. She is of course referring to Watson but, as we know, his first name is John.

So what are we to make of this reference to James? The idea suggested by Dorothy Sayers and championed by Dakin is that Watson's middle name was Hamish and when anglicised it becomes James. The suggestion is that Mary used this rather than call her husband John which would have reminded her of Major John Sholto and consequently the death of her father.

This sounds like a perfectly reasonable theory and has stood the test of time until recently. In the recently published book *Arthur Conan Doyle – A life in Letters*, a letter written by Conan Doyle in March 1908 to H. Greenhough Smith is shown. This letter concerns Conan Doyle's plans for future Holmes stories. The part that is damaging for the Hamish theory is the title he proposes. The title in question is *Reminiscences of Mr Sherlock Holmes (Extracted from the Diaries of his friend Dr James Watson.)* The fact that the name James is used in personal correspondence rather damages the idea that it was a name employed by Mary Morstan to spare herself painful memories. Instead it clearly points to Conan Doyle's tendency to refer to his own characters incorrectly.

The Adventure of the Blue Carbuncle

Published: January 1892
Set in: 1889
Client: None

Synopsis: Watson calls on Holmes to find him examining a battered hat. Holmes explains that a local commissionaire had visited him earlier carrying the hat and a goose that he gained when he attempted to save the original owner from being attacked. Holmes states that he told the commissionaire to keep the goose but retained the hat in order to amuse himself by 'reconstructing' the owner from it.

A short while later the commissionaire returns clutching a huge jewel that his wife discovered in the goose. The jewel turns out to be the famous Blue Carbuncle which had been stolen from its wealthy owner a few days before. Holmes has to solve the mystery of how the gem came to be in the goose and who stole it.

Notes: This story, which Holmes takes on for his own amusement rather than at anyone's behest, ends with Holmes still in possession of the carbuncle. We can assume this as there is no mention of it being handed back to its owner. We are left to hope that he eventually turned it over to the authorities and allowed commissionaire Peterson to claim the reward.

There is a problem with the name of the stone. A carbuncle is a term usually applied to a red gemstone. It is especially associated with garnet. The problems do not end there though. Peterson, the commissionaire who finds the stone, informs Holmes that the stone cuts glass. This therefore is more likely to make the stone a diamond. Perhaps we should just put this down to Conan Doyle not being a gem expert.

The Adventure of the Speckled Band

Published: February 1892
Set in: 1883
Client: Miss Helen Stoner

Synopsis: Helen Stoner visits Holmes and explains that for the past two nights she has been woken by the sound of whistling. It is the same sound that her sister Julia had heard for the few nights preceding her death. This had occurred soon after her engagement was announced and immediately before she died she mentioned a 'speckled band'. Miss Stoner recently announced her own engagement and soon after was moved into her sister's room by their step-father Doctor Roylott. Now that she too is hearing the whistling she has begun to fear for her life.

Notes: In 1927 when Conan Doyle was asked what his favourite stories were, he listed this story as his number one. The villainous (and venomous) snake featured in the story is referred to as the Swamp Adder from India. As many people have noted, there is no such snake. The late Richard Lancelyn Green, former chairman of the Sherlock Holmes Society of London, concluded that the most likely candidate was the Indian cobra or Naja naja. This snake has speckled marks and venom that can lead to death in minutes.

The one aspect of the story that is hard to understand is how no suspicions were aroused by the circumstances of Julia's death. Even if the snake's poison was unknown and therefore undetectable, surely the puncture marks would have raised questions. The idea that they were spotted but deemed irrelevant sounds absurd but it is the only viable alternative to them being missed altogether.

At the beginning of the story Dr Roylott attempts to deter Holmes from involving himself in the case by bending a fire poker with his bare hands. This demonstrated that he clearly had a high opinion of his own ability to intimidate others. The character of Holmes as we know him would never be put off by such aggressive posturing but clearly Roylott thought he would be successful as he made an attempt on the life of his step-daughter soon after. Only an extremely confident or stupid man would do such a thing when aware that a private detective had been consulted and that he was very likely to be a suspect.

The Adventure of the Engineer's Thumb

Published: March 1892
Set in: 1889
Client: Mr Victor Hatherley

Synopsis: Mr Victor Hatherley turns up at Watson's surgery in order to get medical attention for his hand. Watson discovers when he removes the bandage that the man's thumb has been cut off. When told that Hatherley lost it when he was attacked, Watson decides to take him to Holmes for help.

Notes: Dakin points out that the town of Eyford does not exist. He therefore, as expected, suggests that Watson invented the name to cover the true location. He then goes on to try and identify the actual location based on the possible train routes that Hatherley could have taken. Fun as pouring over maps of Berkshire must be it is surely more likely that Conan Doyle invented Eyford and did not base it on any existing location.

The biggest problem concerns the villain Colonel Stark. Having successfully cut off Hatherley's thumb with a cleaver it seems odd that he should make no further effort to finish him off. Hatherley was too dangerous to leave alive so it is curious that Stark's fellow conspirators could have persuaded him to give up the pursuit. It is also to be wondered at that Hatherley managed to make his way back to London so easily. In the time that he was unconscious following the assault he would have lost enough blood to have left him queasy at the very least. However we must defer to Conan Doyle's medical expertise in this area.

The Adventure of the Noble Bachelor

Published: April 1892
Set in: 1888
Client: Lord Robert St. Simon

Synopsis: High society is shocked at the sudden disappearance of Lady St. Simon only hours after her wedding. Lord St. Simon approaches Holmes in the hope that he can find her and discover the reason for her disappearance.

Notes: At the end of this story Holmes displays some pro-American credentials when he says to Francis Moulton that he is always pleased to meet an American and that he one day hopes that the entire world will be united under a single flag which will be a quartering of the Union Jack with the Stars and Stripes. However, as Dakin remarks, we can only hope that Holmes was not advocating the conquest of the world by an Anglo-American alliance. In the present political climate the remark could almost be seen as prophetic.

There is some confusion over the setting of this story. The *New Annotated Sherlock Holmes* has the story set in 1888. However a line in the story remarks that Lord St. Simon was born in 1846 and is forty-one years of age. This would make 1887 more likely but 1888 is not impossible.

In the author's opinion this is one of the dullest stories in the canon. No crime is committed apart from the accidental bigamy of Hatty Doran and it is hardly the stuff of which classic Holmes stories are made.

The Adventure of the Beryl Coronet

Published: May 1892
Set in: 1886
Client: Alexander Holder

Synopsis: Mr Holder, the senior partner in a major bank, comes to Holmes to consult him about the valuable Beryl Coronet that had been left in his keeping as security for a bank loan. Fearing for the safety of the coronet he had taken it home. During the night, after hearing a noise, he had discovered his son, a gambler with large debts, with the coronet in his hands. Convinced of his son's guilt he handed him over to the police but cannot account for the fact that part of the coronet is missing.

Notes: Conan Doyle makes a significant architectural error in the opening line of this story when he refers to Watson as looking out of the Bow window of their sitting room when he sees Holder approaching. Dakin reports that no property with Bow windows existed on the Baker Street of the time. As with many of Conan Doyle's errors, it does not affect the story in any way but it does raise the question of whether Conan Doyle based his description of Holmes and Watson's lodgings on a real building and, if so, was it on Baker Street. The present site of the Sherlock Holmes Museum on Baker Street is sufficiently close to the descriptions given to us by Conan Doyle for us to presume that he did base 221b on a real building even though it is unlikely to be that particular building.

The identity of the 'owner' of the coronet is a subject of debate. Dakin suggests that it could be the Prince of Wales (the future Edward VII). This is primarily suggested because the coronet is referred to as 'One of the most precious public possessions of the empire' by Holder. However it seems unlikely in the extreme that even a member of the Royal Family would find it easy to remove what would be an item from the crown jewels from the Tower of London to use as security for a loan. Also one has to wonder at the purpose for which the loan was required. It is far more likely that the description of the coronet as public property was incorrect and that it was a personal possession of the mysterious client. Another argument against the Prince of Wales theory is that he would be extremely unlikely as the heir to the throne to conduct such business in person. It is more likely, if the client were Royal at all, that he should be a younger son of Queen Victoria and hence more likely to be able to travel incognito and conduct his own business.

The Adventure of the Copper Beeches

Published: June 1892
Set in: 1890
Client: Miss Violet Hunter

Synopsis: Violet Hunter approaches Holmes to seek his opinion about whether or not she should accept a job as governess that she has recently been offered. She is concerned because she has been offered an overly generous salary and because her new employer insists that she cuts her hair short before she can take up the post. Holmes does not make a specific recommendation but offers his help should it be needed.

Holmes and Watson are summoned to see her a short while later and she explains that she has become convinced that someone is being kept prisoner in the house.

Notes: This story marks Conan Doyle's first use of a female character by the name of Violet. He was to use this name a further three times. Violet Smith in *The Solitary Cyclist,* Violet Westbury in *The Bruce-Partington Plans* and Violet De Merville in *The Illustrious Client.*

Dakin decides to offer us a different date to that from other chronologies. While Klinger offers us the date of 1890, Dakin prefers 1885. He bases this on many things including the fact that Watson is described as living at Baker Street and his wife is not mentioned once. However Baring-Gould provides us with the date of 1889, only one year before the date offered by Klinger. He suggests that Watson was indeed unmarried at the time of the case and married Mary Morstan the month following the case. For a change Baring-Gould's idea seems the most appealing.

The Memoirs of Sherlock Holmes

Contains twelve stories published 1892–1893 with original illustrations by Sidney Paget. These stories were commissioned by the *Strand* magazine as a result of the success of the previous twelve stories. The commission for the stories was made by the *Strand* in late January 1892. According to Leslie Klinger's *New Annotated Sherlock Holmes*, Conan Doyle was paid £1000 for this set of stories. The amount is roughly equivalent to £61,000 in today's money. In a letter written by Conan Doyle to his mother in April 1893 he announced his intention to kill Holmes at the end of the series. It is interesting to speculate when he really made this decision. Did he make it at the same time as writing the letter or did he have it in mind at the outset?

Silver Blaze

Published: December 1892
Set in: 1888
Client: Colonel Ross

Synopsis: Colonel Ross calls in Holmes when his champion race horse Silver Blaze goes missing a few days before an important race. In addition the horse's trainer John Straker has been found dead with a massive head wound and cut to his leg a short distance from the stables. Holmes has to find the answer to both mysteries before the race.

Notes: This story is one of two in the canon where the villain of the piece is dead from the very moment the story opens, the other being *The Problem of Thor Bridge*. You will notice the similarity between one of the illustrations from this story and one used in *The Boscombe Valley Mystery*. Once again Paget shows Holmes dressed in the iconic deerstalker.

Silver Blaze is described as being descended from Isonomy who began breeding in 1881. Furthermore Silver Blaze is described as being in his fifth year. Therefore the earliest possible year for the events to take place is 1886. The events pre-date Watson's marriage so must be on or before 1888. This gives us a two year window in which to place this story. Dakin concurs with Klinger setting the year at 1888. The principal reason for this being that Holmes's remark to Watson about his literary efforts must refer to *A Study in Scarlet* which was published in December 1887.

*Watson and Holmes travelling to the scene of the
mystery in The Adventure of Silver Blaze.*

This story contains a good example of Holmes's mischievous nature. When Colonel Ross is dismissive of his abilities Holmes forbids Watson from disclosing any discoveries to him before the Wessex Cup in which Silver Blaze is to take part. He thus leaves Ross wriggling like a worm on a hook before revealing the solution and thoroughly humbling the colonel. He was destined to act in a similar fashion in a number of other stories including *The Mazarin Stone* and *The Norwood Builder.*

The Cardboard Box

Published: January 1893
Set in: 1888
Client: Miss Susan Cushing

Synopsis: Holmes is called in when a spinster receives a cardboard box containing two severed ears. She has led a retired life and does not knowingly have any enemies.

Notes: As we have come to expect, there are theories regarding the date in which the story is set. As with *Silver Blaze*, it is reasonable to assume that it must be set before Watson's marriage as he is clearly living with Holmes. There is no mention of his medical practice or his wife being absent in any way. Therefore the events have to be from 1888 or earlier. So far so good, however the single biggest problem with a date prior to 1888 lies in the fact that, in the conclusion to the story, Holmes makes reference to Watson's accounts of both *A Study in Scarlet* and *The Sign of Four*. It is the latter that makes the dating difficult. The events of *The Sign of Four* took place in 1888 and the account was published in February 1890. If Holmes is able to refer to them both you could infer that the events of the present case are taking place after February 1890. However it then becomes impossible for Watson and Holmes to still be living together as the former would, by this time, have been married for almost two years.

This at first appears to be a serious blow to the 1888 date. However it rather depends on how you choose to interpret Holmes's reference to Watson's accounts. He refers to both as 'chronicled' but he does not say published. Is it not possible that Watson wrote up the events of the Agra treasure soon after they took place? At that point he was only engaged to Mary Morstan and would therefore, as the rules of Victorian society demanded, not yet be living with Mary but still with Holmes. Watson could therefore have completed the account in 1888, allowed Holmes to see it and had it published after the *Cardboard Box*. If we follow this reasoning, a date of late 1888 is once again possible.

Dakin decides to take issue with some of Holmes's remarks in this story. In particular he notes Holmes's account of how he came by his Stradivarius violin. Holmes states that he purchased it from the seller for fifty-five shillings when it was worth five hundred guineas. Dakin suggests that this indicates a lack of morals on Holmes's part. However one has to remember that, if we accept 1888 as the date for the story, it was still early in the collaboration of Holmes and Watson. Holmes was probably still in the position where he found the rent of 221b too much for himself to pay alone. Who under such circumstances would turn their nose up at such a bargain? Many people today believe, rightly or wrongly, that retailers make too much profit at the expense of the consumer. Is it unreasonable to suppose that the same attitude existed in the late nineteenth century? It is a source of constant bewilderment to the present author that other authors are so keen to make Holmes morally perfect and consequently take issue with anything that makes him less so. Does Dakin really think that Holmes would not delight as much as the next person in getting one over a retailer?

The Yellow Face

Published: February 1893
Set in: 1888
Client: Mr Grant Munro

Synopsis: Munro approaches Holmes as he is concerned about the recent activities of his wife. She has been asking him for money without explaining what it is for and she has been paying secret visits to a nearby house. One of the occupants of the house has been seen staring out of the window with a vivid yellow face.

Notes: This is one of the stories set in and around the Norwood area of South London. This story was set in Norbury only a few miles from the area known today as South Norwood. Conan Doyle lived in South Norwood for five years and wrote nearly a third of all the stories during this time.

Commentators who despair of Holmes's language towards Steve Dixie in *The Three Gables* (from the *Casebook*) point to this story as evidence of Holmes's true, and nobler, attitude. The inconsistency in his manner, and the possible reason for it, will be covered in the section that deals with the *Casebook* stories.

One feature of this story that Dakin seizes upon early on is Mrs Munro's references to her husband as Jack rather than Grant. He makes the perfectly reasonable suggestion that this may have been his second name which she may have preferred to use instead of the more formal sounding Grant. While this is an acceptable theory we have only to look at real-life for a similar case. The writer C.S. Lewis was known to his close friends as Jack. This was despite it not being in any way his name. This seems a more likely scenario.

The Stockbroker's Clerk

Published: March 1893
Set in: 1889
Client: Mr Hall Pycroft

Synopsis: The young stockbroker approaches Holmes about the conduct of his new employer. After being made redundant he had secured a well paid job with a London firm. Prior to commencing his employment he had been approached by a man to work for his brother at a different firm in Birmingham at over double the wages. Having been persuaded to accept the post he was further persuaded not to tell the London firm of his change of heart.

After a short while working in Birmingham he has come to Holmes looking for answers. His employment is not very taxing and seems designed purely to keep him occupied for large periods. He is further concerned about the state of the company offices in Birmingham and the fact that he is the only employee apart from his manager.

Notes: This story has significant similarities to *The Red-Headed League*. Both stories feature a man who is duped into taking up a non-existent job in order that he will be out of the way whilst a crime is committed elsewhere.

At the time this story is set Watson and Holmes are living apart as Watson is now in his first year of marriage to Mary Morstan. Furthermore Watson is three months into the running of his medical practice and is busy trying to turn round its fortunes after it had suffered under his predecessor. Holmes drops by to enquire whether he would be interested in being involved in his latest case. It is perhaps a measure of his self-importance that he should expect that Watson would find his case more interesting than his own medical work. Unsurprisingly, Watson is more than willing to accompany Holmes on this new adventure even though it will take him as far away as Birmingham. It is apparently no great inconvenience to Watson to do this as his neighbouring doctor is happy to look after his patients and vice versa. This seems a rather unlikely arrangement. Given that they were working for essentially competing businesses they must have been very trusting of each other to form this arrangement. Surely there would be the temptation for either man to lure away his neighbour's patients permanently. In Watson's case he admits that he is trying to restore the fortunes of his own practice. Surely being absent for days at a time would do it little good. It is also highly dubious that so trusting a bond and arrangement between two competing doctors could have come about in as little as three months.

Mary Morstan's attitude is also of note. As little as three months into their marriage she is very accommodating (to say the least) to allow her husband to just disappear to Birmingham at short notice. We are forced to assume that she must have felt under some obligation to Holmes in the aftermath of *The Sign of Four*. One wonders how long this sense of obligation would have lasted had she not died soon after Holmes's own 'death'.

Hall Pycroft certainly ranks highly as one of Holmes's more observant clients. Even though he finds the offer of employment from Arthur Pinner astounding and asks some pertinent questions he does ultimately accept the post. When he meets Arthur's brother Harry he almost immediately notices the striking similarities between the two and the identical gold teeth convince him that that the two brothers are the same man. Perhaps Pycroft's excellent observations and retelling of events are one of the reasons that Holmes is able to solve the mystery with relatively little exertion.

The 'Gloria Scott'

Published: February 1893
Set in: 1874
Client: None

Synopsis: Holmes's only college friend invites him to stay with him and his father at their home during the summer holiday. During his stay Holmes scares his friend's father by a demonstration of his deductive powers. A short time later a man named Hudson arrives and is promptly employed by his host. Hudson clearly has some hold over the family and Holmes's friend asks him to find out what.

Notes: Holmes's first case, described to Watson. This story has prompted much debate regarding which university Holmes attended. We shall cover the identity of Holmes's university in more depth in our look at *The Three Students.*

As with many stories in the canon there is considerable debate about the date in which this story is set. In fact there are, as Dakin remarks, two dates at issue. The first is the date of Holmes's visit and the second is the date of the voyage of the Gloria Scott. We shall not re-examine those arguments here as they are somewhat comprehensive. The interested reader should obtain a copy of Dakin's book if they wish to explore the matter further (see bibliography).

The interesting chronological aspect that we will look at is the issue of how old Holmes was when he attended university and how long he was there for. Conan Doyle has given contradictory remarks in this area. One of the few stories in the canon about which there is no argument regarding the date is *His Last Bow* which all parties accept is set in 1914. In this story Holmes is described as being sixty years old. Therefore we can say with reasonable certainty that Holmes was born in 1854. Continuing this line of reasoning we can assume that, if he began university at eighteen, he must have commenced his studies in 1872.

So far so good but this is where the inconsistencies begin to creep in. Exactly how long was Holmes at university? At the beginning of this story Holmes tells Watson that Trevor was the only friend he made during his two years at college. This is the only occasion when he states a precise period for his attendance. On other occasions he makes more ambiguous remarks which are open to interpretation. For example, in *The Musgrave Ritual* he refers to his 'last years at the university'. This, as Dakin points out, suggests more than two years. In *The Veiled Lodger* Watson tells us that Holmes was in practice for twenty-three years, seventeen of which involved him. If we count backwards from 1903 when Holmes retired to Sussex it brings us to 1880. However you have to subtract the period during which Holmes was believed to be dead. This, as those familiar with the stories know, was between 1891 and 1894. Subtract these years as well and we arrive at 1877 for the year in which Holmes began his career.

A present day honours degree is awarded after three years academic study perhaps with some form of work experience taking up an additional year. Prior to the mid-twentieth century undergraduates studied for an Ordinary degree and if they performed exceptionally they would be allowed to study an extra year in an attempt to be awarded the degree with honours. The stories leave us in blissful ignorance as to whether Holmes actually completed his degree but it is beyond the realms of belief to accept that Holmes would fail. Baring-Gould is of the opinion that Holmes abandoned his studies in order to pursue his career as a consulting detective. Assuming he did this after the two years that he referred to it means he did so right at the point where he might have actually been awarded his Ordinary degree. The present author prefers to think that Holmes did in fact obtain his degree and then, like many a present-day graduate, decided to pursue an unrelated career. However we now have three years to account for. The two years of study bring us to 1874 and we need to get to 1877. It is presumably this gap that has led to the idea that Holmes attended both Oxford and Cambridge. Baring-Gould suggests that, after spending a short period of time at St Bartholomew's Hospital in London studying Chemistry, Holmes studied medicine and natural sciences at Gonville and Caius College and furthermore that it was at Cambridge that he met Reginald Musgrave. Dakin objects to this idea believing that someone from an aristocratic background like Musgrave would instinctively have gone to Oxford. Even today there is a perception that Oxford is superior although it is not quite clear on what this perception is based. Assuming it was just as strong a perception then, Dakin's position seems the most reasonable.

Another possibility is that Holmes may have commenced University at an older age than eighteen. If, for the sake of argument, we assume that Holmes commenced University at twenty years old he could have spent two years at Oxford (or Cambridge) and then, with or without degree, moved to London for chemistry study at St Bartholomew's before formally beginning his practice.

The Musgrave Ritual

Published: May 1893
Set in: 1879
Client: Sir Reginald Musgrave

Synopsis: Brunton, the butler of Hurlstone vanishes two days after his dismissal by his employer Reginald Musgrave. Three days later one of the maids, Rachel Howells, to whom Brunton had once been engaged, also vanishes.

Musgrave, who was at university with Holmes, comes to ask for his advice on the matter. He reveals that Brunton had been dismissed for looking at a private family paper entitled 'The Musgrave Ritual'. After reading the paper Holmes becomes convinced that it refers to a location on the Musgrave estate and he travels there in an effort to solve both the riddle and the disappearances.

Notes: This the second of Holmes's pre-Watson cases. It opens with Watson complaining to Holmes about the untidy state of their lodgings. In response to this accusation, Holmes produces a large box in which he has kept records of his previous cases. Watson immediately becomes fascinated with the contents of the box which leads to Holmes telling him the story of the case.

The many anomalies with this story are well covered by Dakin. We shall however join him in questioning why the Musgrave treasure was not found before. As Dakin points out, the treasure was kept in a cellar commonly used for storing wood. Therefore this would be a room likely to receive regular visitors, especially during the winter months. The idea that no one would have ever raised the flagstone to see what was under it stretches credibility.

However the most interesting aspect of this story does not concern the events of the case itself but the other case notes that Holmes states are also contained within his box.

Dakin makes special reference to the case listed as the adventure of 'Ricoletti of the club foot and his abominable wife'. In yet another swipe at the character of Watson, Dakin suggests that it is conceivable that Holmes actually said 'wrinkled yeti' and 'abominable life'. This is based purely on the similarity of the sound of 'Ricoletti' and 'wrinkled yeti' and the use of the word 'abominable'. The suggestion that Holmes solved the mystery of the abominable snowman is rather fanciful to say the least. The idea actually puts Dakin in similar territory to Baring-Gould who suggested that Holmes was a cousin of Conan Doyle's other creation - Professor Challenger of *The Lost World* - and that Holmes was involved in the capture of a live Pterodactyl that Challenger is supposed to have brought back from his adventures to exhibit. When Dakin came up with his idea he would have done well to remember his own assessment of Baring-Gould's Jack the Ripper / Athelney Jones theory as an '... outré flight of fancy...'

The Reigate Squires

Published: June 1893
Set in: 1887
Client: Surry Police

Synopsis: At Watson's suggestion Holmes has travelled with him to Surrey to stay with his friend Colonel Hayter. During their stay they hear of a robbery which has taken place at the nearby Acton estate in which a number of bizarre, non-valuable items have been stolen. Later they hear of a murder at the nearby Cunningham estate where the victim was the coachman.

Notes: This story highlights how the police tend to be more respectful of Holmes the further away from London the cases take place. In London the likes of Lestrade are always hoping to score points and beat Holmes to the answers. You have only to read *The Norwood Builder* for evidence of this. In this story Inspector Forrester is positively delighted to find that Holmes is in the area and specifically asks for his assistance in solving the murder of the coachman.

The gun that killed William Kirwan is worthy of examination. When Alec Cunningham attempts to use the gun after being caught in the act of attempting to kill Holmes Inspector Forrester knocks it from his hand. Holmes remarks that it will be useful at the trial. One is compelled to ask how? With the technology of the time there was no way to positively match the gun to the bullet. No fingerprints could have been retrieved as the practice had not yet been adopted. The most you could demonstrate was that the gun fired the same kind of bullets.

The letter that Holmes states was written by both Cunninghams is decidedly odd. Holmes remarks that they distrusted each other and were both determined to have an equal hand in events. Even if such distrust did exist there was no need for both of them to write the letter. One could have simply watched the other write the note thus ensuring that they were both aware of what was written.

Finally we have Annie Morrison whose name features in the note that was sent to William Kirwan. Who was she? Her name appears nowhere else in the story and Holmes shows no apparent interest in finding out. One possible interpretation is that Kirwan and Annie wanted to marry but lacked the money to do so. Kirwan may have seen blackmail as a means to make such a marriage happen. Alas there is no way to prove this theory.

The Crooked Man

Published: July 1893
Set in: 1889
Client: Major Murphy of the Royal Mallows

Synopsis: Colonel James Barclay is found dead in his home with a look of horror on his face. His wife Nancy is found unconscious in the same room. The police consider her the prime suspect as the room was locked and the serving staff had heard a violent argument between the two earlier in the evening. Holmes's interest is particularly aroused by the fact that the key to the room has not been found.

Notes: After *The Sign of Four* this is the second story to have a background based around the British Army in India.

Once again we have a case that illustrates how tolerant Watson's wife Mary is. As before, we have Holmes just popping round and dragging Watson off on another case. However Watson's army background would have no doubt been useful to Holmes on a case such as this.

The story is very illustrative of how love can blind a person to their own best interests. Barclay sacrifices his friend Henry Wood to the enemy purely to remove him as a rival to Nancy's affections. However Wood was on a mission to link up with reinforcements to save the soldiers and wives of his garrison. Barclay was risking not only his and Nancy's lives but also his entire garrison purely because of his infatuation. In this case the reinforcements made it without Wood's assistance but there was no way that Barclay could know that in advance.

There is little argument about the date in which this story is set with most placing it in 1889. This is mostly due to the fact that Watson is in the first few months of his marriage which places the case in early 1889 at the earliest. Dakin also bases the 1889 date on the fact that the Indian Mutiny ended in 1858 and Colonel and Mrs Barclay had been married since then or shortly after. Coupled with Mrs Barclay's remark that she thought Henry Wood had been dead for thirty years puts the date easily in 1888 / 1889. It is Watson's references to his own marriage then nudge us firmly into 1889.

Klinger remarks that this story belongs to the classic locked room genre of crime. The other stories in the canon that fall comfortably into this category are *The Speckled Band* and *The Empty House*.

The Resident Patient

Published: August 1893
Set in: 1887
Client: Mr Blessington and Dr Percy Trevelyan.

Synopsis: Dr Trevelyan approaches Holmes about Mr Blessington who is the resident patient at his London surgery. Some months previously Blessington had approached Trevelyan and offered to finance his medical work in exchange for being allowed to live with him and have him as his personal doctor. Despite the unusual terms of the offer, Trevelyan had agreed. The arrangement had gone well until one day when Blessington had become extremely agitated about a burglary and demanded that the surgery be fitted with the latest locks, bolts and other security measures. Over the following days Blessington had become more and more scared and anxious and had ultimately demanded that Holmes be consulted when he became convinced there had been intruders in his room.

Holmes interviews Blessington but walks out when he becomes convinced that Blessington is lying to him. The next day Blessington is discovered hanging in his room. The police initially suspect suicide but Holmes is convinced that the evidence all points to an execution.

Notes: This story shares a similarity with *The Five Orange Pips* in that the perpetrators manage to elude Holmes, despite being identified, but are presumed lost when their ship sinks.

Moving on to the date, most sources place the events in 1887. Holmes reports that the Worthington bank gang were jailed in 1875 for fifteen years each with the exception of Cartwright who was hanged. If they had served their full term they would have been released in 1890. Holmes remarks that they were released some years before their full term but does not state how many years early this was. Dakin mentions the theory held by most other sources that they were released three-and-a-half years early although it is not clear how this amount was arrived at. He goes on to take a different approach to the date. He refers to Watson's remark at the beginning of the original story as published in the *Strand*. This version, which differs from those published subsequently, has Watson stating that the events took place towards the end of the first year that he shared rooms with Holmes. This would make the date 1881. The problem with this is that it would mean that the Worthington bank gang were released after serving only six years of their fifteen year sentence. Such an early release is clearly impossible for such a crime. Dakin tries to get round this by inferring that the gang were actually convicted and sentenced in 1870 rather than 1875 and that Watson had written down the wrong date. This is rather unlikely however given that Watson would have had access to Holmes's press cuttings regarding the trial. Therefore the date of 1887 really should be allowed to stand. The fact that the text suggesting the earlier date was removed after the original publication suggests that the mistake was spotted and removed (presumably at Conan Doyle's request.)

The Greek Interpreter

Published: September 1893
Set in: 1888
Client: Mr Melas

Synopsis: Mr Melas talks to Holmes about his visit to a remote house where he was forced to interpret for a kidnapped Greek man who was being held against his will and who was only allowed to communicate by means of chalk and a small blackboard.

Notes: This is the first story in which Mycroft Holmes features. The scene at the Diogenes Club in which Mycroft and Holmes analyse the former solider and his circumstances is clearly done purely to back up Holmes assertion that Mycroft is the smarter and more observant of the two. Regrettably it is rather contrived as one cannot conceive of Holmes making the mistake that he does under normal circumstances.

The villains of the story actually elude Holmes due to delays with obtaining a warrant but ultimately meet their end months later in Hungary. This rather unsatisfying and mysterious ending has been hijacked by Baring-Gould who once again makes Moriarty the brains behind the scheme. He infers that some greater authority must have brought the villains Latimer and Kemp together and that Moriarty may have brought about their subsequent deaths.

Turning to the date, Klinger and Baring-Gould place the date of the case in 1888. It certainly cannot be any later as Watson moves out to return to practice soon after and he is clearly living with Holmes in this story. Dakin however chooses to opt for 1884. This dating is actually based on remarks made by Holmes in *The Bruce-Partington Plans*. Holmes elaborates on his brother Mycroft's true position in the Government and tells Watson that he did not explain more fully at the time of the *Greek Interpreter* because he did not know Watson so well. Dakin infers from this remark that the case must have taken place soon after they first met in 1881. The problem with this, as Dakin himself acknowledges, is that Watson opens the account remarking on his 'long and intimate acquaintance' with Sherlock Holmes. Such a remark would not be made after only one or two years. In view of this Dakin plumps for 1884 as a kind of mid-way date between 1881 and 1888.

The Naval Treaty

Published: October 1893
Set in: 1889
Client: Percy Phelps

Synopsis: Holmes is called in to help Percy Phelps, a former school friend of Watson, who works at the Foreign Office. An important Naval Treaty which was in his keeping has gone missing from his office and he is the prime suspect. Despite the theft happening over nine weeks previously and the high value of the treaty to foreign powers there has been no word of it.

Notes: Watson refers to two other cases at the commencement of this story that all supposedly occurred in the same July. They are *The Adventure of the Second Stain* and *The Adventure of the Tired Captain*. Only the former of these was subsequently written by Conan Doyle and it raises an interesting question of chronology. In *The New Annotated Sherlock Holmes* the timeline lists *The Naval Treaty* as taking place in 1889 and *The Second Stain* as taking place in 1894. This puts the former story before the events preceding Holmes's 'death' in *The Final Problem* and the latter story after his return in *The Empty House*. This is rather at odds with Watson's statement that they took place in not only the same year but the same month. The fact that he refers to them happening in the July after his marriage to, presumably, Mary Morstan means that *The Second Stain* must have occurred in 1889 as Watson would most likely have married Mary Morstan sometime during 1888 or early 1889.

Conan Doyle, as we've come to expect, subsequently contradicted himself in the opening of *The Second Stain* when he referred to the events as taking place '… upon one Tuesday morning in autumn'. July is not in the autumn. Due to the sensitive nature of the case Watson does not provide any further chronological details. This has given rise to the idea that there was more than one case of the same name. We shall look more into the dating of *The Second Stain* later.

Of particular interest is the confrontation between Inspector Forbes and Holmes. During their initially heated discussion Holmes reveals that the police have had all the credit in forty-nine of his last fifty-three cases. Only twenty-five cases from the entire canon are set in or before this year (according to Klinger's chronology) and the only published case at this time would have been *A Study in Scarlet*. Assuming this was one of the four cases in which Holmes's name featured (and it is perfectly possible that it was not) one can but wonder what the other three cases were where Holmes did not see fit not to hand the initial credit over to Scotland Yard as was his custom.

The Final Problem

Published: December 1893
Set in: 1891
Client: None

Synopsis: Holmes arrives at Watson's surgery superficially wounded from a fight with a hired thug. In response to Watson's questions he explains that he has been laying plans for the arrest of Professor Moriarty, the greatest criminal brain of the century, and that it is the Professor who is responsible for him being attacked. Holmes asks Watson to travel to Europe with him for the few days before the arrest can take place. As they travel they are pursued by Moriarty.

Notes: Watson reports the death of Holmes at the end of the story. The reaction among the general public bordered on hysteria. Many people took to wearing black armbands as a sign of mourning, angry letters were sent to Conan Doyle and a considerable number of people cancelled their subscriptions to the *Strand* in protest.

The Granada television series opened this episode with Holmes in France, at the request of the French Government, recovering the Mona Lisa after its theft from the Louvre. This was clearly done to provide the audience with a specific motive for Moriarty's appearance and attempted vengeance. The original story also states that Holmes was working in France on behalf of the French Government but it does not state precisely what he had been engaged to do.

Much time has been spent by other Sherlockian scholars on this story and *The Empty House,* these being the two stories that mark the beginning and end of what is known as 'The

Great Hiatus'. We shall address some of the issues around the latter story later on. It has to be remembered that Conan Doyle's intention was to finish Holmes off at the end of the story. As previously discussed, the sole purpose of creating Professor Moriarty was to create a character that was capable of defeating Holmes. Hence Moriarty's entire biography was sketched out by Holmes to Watson at the beginning of the story. He needed to be fleshed out as soon as possible in order for the reader to be convinced of his ability to beat Holmes.

Much has been made of what some scholars refer to as Watson's inconsistency when he claims not to have heard of Moriarty when asked by Holmes. The chronologies put forward by both Dakin and *The New Annotated Sherlock Holmes* give a date of 1891 for the events of the story. Yet, in the opening pages of *The Valley of Fear*, a conversation between Holmes and Watson reveals that Watson is well acquainted with Moriarty, referring to him as 'The famous scientific criminal'. To many scholars this is an issue because the same chronologies set this story in 1888, before the events of *The Final Problem*. At first glance this does indeed look bad but it has to be borne in mind that *The Valley of Fear* was published in 1914, nearly twenty years after *The Final Problem*. The mistake here is Conan Doyle's rather than Watson's and only serves to highlight once again the bizarre tendency amongst some authors to blame Watson for mistakes as if Conan Doyle intentionally made him a bad or misleading chronicler. When he wrote this story he had no intention of Holmes ever emerging from the Reichenbach Falls. When he did finally bow to pressure and resurrect him he was, to all intents and purposes, starting with a blank canvas as he had never intended to write anything further about Holmes. It is true that he left the door open for a return by making it clear that Holmes's body was not found but we can be reasonably confident that he hoped Holmes would be allowed to die in order that he could get on with his more 'important' writing. When he wrote *The Valley of Fear* and decided to make Moriarty a feature of it he was making a mistake that he must have realised would have been seized upon. Perhaps he simply did not care about the inconsistency; after all he was destined to be consistently inconsistent throughout the series. An example of this is seen with *The Second Stain* which we are yet to examine.

Holmes and Moriarty meet in The Final Problem

Holmes's final letter to Watson, which the latter finds at the Reichenbach Falls, contains one very interesting reference. Holmes refers to his career as being in crisis and how his own death, as long as it accompanied Moriarty's, would be 'congenial'. It is interesting to speculate as to how he reached this negative conclusion. If you assume that his career began with *The Gloria Scott* in 1874 it means his career had, by that time, been going for seventeen years. Immediately after learning via telegram that Moriarty had eluded the police he remarks to Watson that he has worked on a thousand cases. Doing simple calculations here reveals that he must have had, on average, fifty-eight cases a year or just over one a week. We can assume this total to be correct given Holmes's remark in *The Greek Interpreter* about the equal evils of modesty and bragging:

'... To the logician all things should be seen exactly as they are, and to underestimate one's self is as much a departure from truth as to exaggerate one's own powers.'

Therefore the 'crisis' cannot be due to a lack of work unless you take issue with the figures and put them down to either Watson's bad recollection or Conan Doyle's mistake. The issue of money then needs to be addressed. Was Holmes struggling with the rent in Watson's absence? Watson at this time was married and living in Paddington. Were the rooms that were 'too much for his purse' still too costly? The answer to this question, if you look at the canon as a whole, is a resounding no. In *The Dying Detective* which, according to most chronologies, is set in 1890 before the events of *The Final Problem*, Watson states that Holmes was so wealthy that he would have been able to purchase his rooms in Baker Street if he so chose. This statement does not entirely lay the ghost of money to rest. *The Dying Detective* was published in 1913, twenty years after *The Final Problem*. Therefore it is entirely possible that, at the time of writing, Conan Doyle had decided that money troubles would be the 'crisis' to which Holmes was referring.

The only other crisis that is plausible is the possibility that Holmes felt a sense of failure when his carefully laid plans failed to result in Moriarty's arrest. However he could hardly have been surprised at this when he knew that Moriarty had pursued him from London to the coast and would certainly follow him onto the continent.

The Hound of the Baskervilles

Published: August 1901 – April 1902
Set in: 1889
Client: Sir Henry Baskerville

Synopsis: Dr Mortimer approaches Holmes and Watson about the recent death of Sir Charles Baskerville and the legend of the Hound of the Baskervilles. He seeks Holmes's guidance about how he should protect Sir Henry Baskerville who, as Sir Charles' nephew and heir, will inherit both the estate and the curse.

Notes: This was the first adventure written after Holmes's death in *The Final Problem* and was dated prior to the events of that story. Conan Doyle had been inspired to write the story after a holiday in Dartmoor with his friend Bertram Fletcher Robinson, a correspondent for the *Daily Express*. A discussion about local legends involving spectral hounds appealed to Conan Doyle, whose personal interest in all matters of the spirit world was already established although not widely known, and he decided that it would be the good basis for a story.

The Hound of the Baskervilles

Its publication was a cause of both joy and sorrow amongst the legions of fans who had been left without their hero for eight years since the publication of *The Final Problem* in 1893. It was also in many respects a good way of ascertaining the public's appetite for further Holmes adventures, although this probably did not concern Conan Doyle at the time. The story was published in the *Strand* in a series of monthly parts between August 1901 and April 1902 and its publication went some way to restoring the fortunes of the magazine. The readers that had been lost in the aftermath of Holmes's death flooded back to read the latest adventure. During this period Holmes's profile was further raised thanks to William Gillette who was starring as Holmes in *Sherlock Holmes - A Drama in Four Acts*. The play, which had already enjoyed a successful run in the United States, debuted on September 9th 1901 at the Lyceum Theatre, London.

In his book, Dakin discusses at length the issue of the date assigned to the story, referring to it as '...one of the most puzzling in the Canon'. The whole story opens with Holmes and Watson's discussion about the stick left behind by Dr Mortimer. The date inscribed on it states that it was presented in 1884 and Holmes remarks that this was five years ago. Hence the perfectly logical date of 1889 is ascribed to the events of the story thus making it clear that it predates the events of *The Final Problem*. W.S. Baring-Gould in his book, *Sherlock Holmes – A biography of the world's first consulting detective*, puts forward the date of 1888 and this was echoed by Matthew Bunson in *The Sherlock Holmes Encyclopaedia*.

Now you might ask what great difference this one year makes. In fact the one year is highly significant. If you stick with 1889 you have one very big problem and it concerns Watson's marriage. Watson is married by the end of 1888 or early 1889 after the events of *The Sign of Four* so in 1889 he would not be a resident at Baker Street. Despite this he refers to Dr Mortimer as 'our' visitor in the opening paragraph of the story, giving the clear impression that he does still reside with Holmes. Pushing the date back one year to 1888 goes a long way towards removing this problem. Dakin decides to go the other way and expresses his own preference for 1899 but, on the grounds of the dates of Watson's letters to Holmes during the story and the calendars of the time, decides to settle on 1900.

The clear problem with this however is that this places the events after Holmes's return from the dead in *The Empty House*. It stretches credibility to breaking point to suggest that Watson would, as it were, reintroduce Holmes to his adoring public and not explain the circumstances of his 'resurrection', which would surely be of the utmost importance to his fans, until his following account.

However, once again, the cause of all these problems is more likely to be Conan Doyle rather than Watson. He wrote the story and published it in 1901. Perhaps, in the eight years that had elapsed since the last story was published, he had genuinely forgotten to take into account how his chosen date would be out of place with the previous stories. Given the speed with which he produced all of the stories it is surely more than possible that a lot of the inconsistencies scholars dwell on arise from this almost production line speed. We must also accept the fact that the story could have so easily been one without Holmes.

At the time that Conan Doyle was seized with the desire to weave a story around the legends of Dartmoor Holmes was already dead at the bottom of the Reichenbach Falls. We have no way of knowing how much of the story had been plotted out before the decision to include Holmes was made. We can argue that it was simply the desire to avoid having to invent new characters and perhaps the desire to guarantee large sales that prompted him to use Holmes. It was clearly his intention that this would be a one-off story as the resurrection of Holmes was still two years away and not something that Conan Doyle had yet considered. Hence, despite all the inconsistencies we really ought to leave this story in 1889 as written or push it back into the tail end of 1888.

The Return of Sherlock Holmes

Contains thirteen stories published 1903–1904 with original illustrations by Sidney Paget. Sadly Paget died in 1908 four years after the publication of the last of the series. At the time of his death he had produced 356 illustrations for the series and had set the standard for all future illustrators.

According to letters in *Arthur Conan Doyle – A life in Letters,* Conan Doyle was persuaded to resurrect Holmes by Norman Hapgood, by that time editor of *Collier's Weekly*, an American magazine. In his letter Conan Doyle reveals that he was offered $25,000 for the American rights to a mere six stories increasing to $45,000 for thirteen stories. This was the number that Conan Doyle eventually wrote. We must not lose sight of the fact that this was purely for the American rights. The rights in Britain and the rest of the world would have increased this amount considerably.

The Adventure of the Empty House

Published: October 1903
Set in: 1894
Client: Scotland Yard

Synopsis: The body of Ronald Adair, the second son of a prominent diplomat, is found shot in a locked room. The murder has the police and public baffled. Watson and Inspector Lestrade are both involved in the case but are struggling to make any progress.

Notes: Following the success of *The Hound of the Baskervilles* Conan Doyle was fully aware that there was still sufficient public interest in Holmes (if he ever doubted it). However he was not moved to write further adventures until the offer from *Collier's Weekly*. The considerable amount of money involved caused Conan Doyle to give way and he formally resurrected Holmes in this story. As a result the tale is largely devoted to Holmes's reappearance and explanation to Watson about his faked death and travels since the events of *The Final Problem*. The murder of Ronald Adair is very much the secondary element of the tale and hence is devoid of the usual level of investigation and deduction that is displayed in the other adventures. After this story Conan Doyle was to produce over thirty more adventures contained in *The Return of Sherlock Holmes, His Last Bow, The Valley of Fear* and *The Casebook of Sherlock Holmes*.

It has been remarked that there is a problem with this story which stems from Holmes's explanation for faking his death. He states to Watson that Colonel Moran, who was Moriarty's second-in-command, had seen him survive the confrontation and had tried to kill him immediately afterwards by hurling large rocks at him. Therefore, it has been argued, if Moran knew Holmes was alive what was to be gained by pretending to be dead to the world at large. This is a fair question as all the time the world believed Holmes to be dead Moran would have been able to kill him with minimal fear of the law catching up with him. After all how can you kill someone who is already dead?

Holmes's reason for pretending to be dead could be presumed to be as follows. If he was no longer appearing in the media and no longer being discussed in society it would have been virtually impossible to keep a track on his activities, especially as he would not be using his own name. It should be remembered that in *The Final Problem* Holmes received a message from England, presumably from the Inspector Patterson to whom he alluded in his 'final' letter to Watson, to say that all the members of Moriarty's gang had been arrested with the exception of Moriarty himself. Leaving aside the obvious discrepancy that he, Moran, was also at large, it would mean that Moran would have had few allies to rely upon in his search for Holmes. Any such allies would know from Moran that Holmes was alive but they would have little or no idea as to his location. This would have facilitated Holmes's plan to wait for the right circumstances to present themselves for him to come out of hiding and bring about Moran's arrest.

Dakin puts forward the theory that Holmes's tale of his absence was in fact fiction and that perhaps Holmes had a breakdown in Florence after eluding Moran. He is one amongst many who suggest the idea that the story of Holmes's travels is a false one. The best we can do here is to return to the text of the story. It is clear that Holmes never intended to stay away for as long as he did. In his explanation to Watson he mentions that he followed the progress of the trial in which Moriarty's gang were the accused. If he was able to monitor the trial so closely he must have been geographically close perhaps still in Florence or possibly in France. The news that two of the gang were acquitted was no doubt the motivation for the extended leave of absence. Was Moran one of these two acquitted men? The first instinct would be to say no as Moran was out of the country at the time of the arrests alluded to in the telegram.

Could he have been arrested on his return to England? It is an interesting question that is not tackled. Presumably the papers that Holmes left behind for Inspector Patterson contained evidence against Moran that would have justified his arrest. A reasonable conclusion to draw is that Moran returned to England, was arrested but subsequently acquitted. Holmes said that the trial left two of his most vindictive enemies at liberty. If Moran had not been part of the trial Holmes would have surely said that three of his enemies were at large. Having said all that it seems strange that Moran would have returned to England except under a false name as Moriarty is sure to have warned him of the danger of his arrest.

During his extended and presumably unexpected time away from England, Holmes travelled to many places. Dakin cautions us against accepting Holmes's official account of his visits to Lhasa or Khartoum on the grounds that they would have been extremely difficult to accomplish at the time. Here you have to allow for dramatic licence on the part of Conan Doyle. Whilst it undoubtedly helps with authenticity, it is not necessary for the adventures of Holmes to always dovetail with known history. The habit of merging reality and fantasy is a device of many authors. Why should we assume Conan Doyle to be any different?

Dakin's suggestion that Holmes actually spent his time in a nursing home is somewhat unlikely. He refers, in his conversation with Watson, to the journeys of Sigerson as his own and states that Watson may have read of them. The clear implication here is that they appeared in the international press.

In this event Holmes is either being truthful or he is taking the credit for someone else's achievements. Not only would the latter be uncharacteristic it would also be very easy to discover. Watson was undoubtedly hurt by the faked death and extended absence. Would Holmes really have made this worse by stating a lie that would be relatively easy to uncover?

Lastly we must look at Colonel Moran's fate. There must have presumably been something amiss at the Adair trial because Moran was not hung. As Blakeney reports, Moran was clearly still alive at the time of *The Adventure of the Illustrious Client* as Holmes refers to him being alive in his conversation with Sir James Damery. Murder was a capital offence so it must have been decided to charge Moran with a lesser offence which would have merited life imprisonment.

The Adventure of the Norwood Builder

Published: November 1903
Set in: 1894
Client: John Hector MacFarlane

Synopsis: Jonas Oldacre, a retired builder living in Lower Norwood, goes missing. Charred remains are found burning in an outbuilding and are identified as his by the housekeeper thanks to some trouser buttons. John MacFarlane approaches Holmes for help as he is the prime suspect thanks to Oldacre making him the sole beneficiary of his will the previous day.

Notes: Oldacre is described in this story as being a resident of Lower Norwood. The areas known as Lower Norwood, Upper Norwood and South Norwood are situated in present-day South East London and were created as a result of enclosure acts. These acts split the area known as the Great North Wood, hence the name Norwood. However, while Upper Norwood and South Norwood still carry the same names today, Lower Norwood became known as West Norwood on or about 1885. Conan Doyle published this story in 1903 and many sources agree that it was set in 1894. Both dates are some time after the renaming of the area to West Norwood. While many locals of the time would have probably still referred to the area as Lower Norwood, you would expect an official such as Inspector Lestrade to refer to the area by its modern name if only for the purpose of official records.

This case is also noteworthy as it is one where Holmes actually starts to believe that Lestrade has the upper hand. This sorry state of affairs only alters upon the discovery of a bloodied thumb print in Oldacre's hall which Holmes recalls was not there the previous day when he first examined the area. The use of a thumbprint raises questions. At the time of the story's publication, fingerprinting was very much a new weapon in the police armoury. In 1880 Dr Henry Faulds had published a paper on fingerprints in *Nature*, the scientific journal. He approached Scotland Yard about using fingerprint identification but was rebuffed. Sir Francis Galton, a relative of Charles Darwin, later decided to look into the idea. However he chose to do so independently without making any use of Faulds' work. In 1888 he published a Royal Institution Paper on the subject and followed this up with his book *Fingerprints* in 1892. In the book Galton set out his own method for the identification and classification of fingerprints. The paper and subsequent book were the first to give the subject a scientific base and this no doubt helped with the credibility of the whole idea of fingerprint identification. Despite this nine further years elapsed before Great Britain's first fingerprint bureau was opened at Scotland Yard in 1901.

We can be reasonably confident that Conan Doyle knew about this development when he wrote the story as Lestrade tells Holmes about the theory that no two fingerprints are alike when they examine the bloody thumbprint in Oldacre's hall. Holmes sarcastically feigns a lack of knowledge on the subject but is clearly well acquainted with the theory.

This is where the problem arises. One can easily imagine a man such as Holmes reading Galton's book on fingerprints as soon as it was published in 1892. He may even have been the kind of person who would have obtained a copy of the original paper in 1888 or indeed have read Faulds' earlier paper of 1880. However would Lestrade really have had the foresight to read up on the subject before it came into use at Scotland Yard? If the suggested setting of 1894 is correct it would be seven years before fingerprints could be used as evidence in England.

Even if he had read up on the subject he would not have wasted time on a piece of evidence that he could not necessarily use.

This story marks Watson's return to Baker Street full-time. He outlines at the beginning of the story how a Dr Verner had bought his medical practice and how he had subsequently found that Verner was relation of Holmes and that Holmes had actually provided the money. Watson also states that during the time the events of the story took place he was banned by Holmes from making the details of his cases public and that the account was only being released now that the ban had been lifted.

The final comment has to be reserved for the charred remains found at Oldacre's house and identified as his by the housekeeper. Dakin questions how the police could have failed to determine that the remains were not human and thus clear McFarlane very early on. The answer to this question lies in the story itself. The reference to charred remains is made in the newspaper report that Watson reads to Holmes at the beginning of the story. However, at the end of the story, when Holmes asks Oldacre what he really burned in the fire, he refers to charred ashes. It can be stated with some confidence that Holmes is more likely to be accurate than a sensational newspaper report. With the technology of the time it would have been difficult if not impossible to determine the identity of any living thing purely from its ashes. Therefore this seems the most probable answer to Dakin's question.

The Adventure of the Dancing Men

Published: December 1903
Set in: 1898
Client: Mr Hilton Cubitt

Synopsis: Cubitt approaches Holmes about a fear that has come over his young American wife Nancy. She has been living in terror since a letter from America arrived some weeks previously and mysterious messages consisting entirely of matchstick men are appearing around their house and grounds. Despite her evident terror she refuses to discuss the subject with him.

Notes: Along with The Five Orange Pips this is one of the rare cases where Holmes's client dies before the case is solved.

As Dakin remarks, Mrs Cubitt was unreasonable in the extreme in being unwilling to discuss her past with her husband. All the time they were left alone there was no harm in it but the moment the letter arrived she should have told her husband everything. Had she done so it would have saved all concerned considerable time and trouble and her husband almost certainly would have avoided being slain.

It is doubtful whether Abe Slaney really came to England to win Elsie back as he claimed. It was her dislike of her father's criminal activities that caused her to flee America. He would have been well aware that his continued membership of the gang would have not induced her to fly with him. Therefore he was either deluded about his chances of success or he had no intention of luring her away. Slaney states in his interview that it was only after Elsie's marriage that he was able to locate her. This admission needs to be examined. Slaney knew that she had fled to England and presumably what port she would have arrived at but beyond that he would have had no idea where to look. It is possible that he could have liaised with members of the English criminal underworld but there is no evidence within the story for this. If he was so convinced that Elsie wanted to be with him he would surely have never entertained the idea that she would marry someone else. The wedding of a relatively insignificant Norfolk squire would not have been headline news in the national press so he must have been in the habit of reading the wedding notices specifically. This suggests that he had accepted the idea that she may have married and this implies that it was more for pure vengeance than any hope of reconciliation that he pursued her to Norfolk. You might suppose that he intended to kill Cubitt and take Elsie away but he must have realised that this would not have aided his cause. If you add to all this the message 'Elsie prepare to meet thy God' it seems pretty clear that his intentions were far from romantic.

The Adventure of the Solitary Cyclist

Published: January 1904
Set in: 1895
Client: Violet Smith

Synopsis: Miss Smith works in Farnham, Surrey for a Mr Carruthers as music teacher to his daughter. One evening at Carruthers' home, she found herself the object of unwanted attention from one Mr Woodley, an associate of Carruthers. After a brief scuffle between the two men she was promised by Carruthers that she would not be bothered further.

On the occasion of her first visit to town after these events she noticed that she was being followed along a short stretch of road, to and from the railway station, by a solitary cyclist.

Notes: The date is quite clearly wrong. Watson states that Violet Smith visited Baker Street on Saturday 23rd April 1895. As Dakin points out, in 1895 the 23rd of April fell on a Tuesday. Dakin's instinct therefore is to move the date back to the 13th which was a Saturday and this seems a sensible move. As to the reason for the error we need only look at the calendar for 1904, the year of publication. In 1904, April 23rd was a Saturday so it seems pretty clear that Conan Doyle was looking at his current calendar when he was writing the story.

Whilst the plot is clever it is entirely beyond plausibility. It was well known that a marriage conducted against the will of any of the involved parties would be invalid. How Carruthers and Woodley expected a forced marriage by an unfrocked priest on unlicensed ground to aid them in their quest to obtain Ralph Smith's money is anyone's guess.

The Adventure of the Priory School

Published: February 1904
Set in: 1901
Client: Duke of Holderness

Synopsis: Lord Saltire, the son and heir of the Duke of Holderness, goes missing from his boarding school. The German master goes missing at the same time and is presumed to be the abductor. Dr Huxtable, the headmaster of the school, comes to Holmes to seek his help in the recovery of the child. Holmes, having taken on the case, initially cannot understand the minimal cooperation from the Duke.

Notes: We see here how Holmes is not afraid to tell his social superiors where they have erred. The Duke was powerful enough to crush Holmes if he so chose but despite this Holmes was able to reprimand him for his lack of action without any reprisal.

The doubling by the Duke of his fee from six thousand pounds to twelve thousand pounds has been taken by some as an attempt to bribe Holmes into keeping silent about the Duke's complicity in his son's abduction. Admittedly it is hard to see it any other way. Under the circumstances the Duke would have had to throw a great deal of money about to prevent the facts coming out. While James Wilder would keep quiet knowing that a prison term would await him if he spoke out, Reuben Hayes would unfailingly go to the gallows for the death of the German master. As many have pointed out, it is hard to imagine that he would remain quiet about the whole affair. Holmes's suggestion that the Duke could persuade him to remain quiet is ludicrous. A man facing death has nothing to lose. Only if the

Duke had the power to have the sentence commuted to life imprisonment would Hayes have any reason to keep quiet. It is highly unlikely that the Duke would have such power.

These facts aside this is one of the best stories from *The Return of Sherlock Holmes* and one of the author's personal favourites.

The Adventure of Black Peter

Published: March 1904
Set in: 1895
Client: Scotland Yard

Synopsis: Inspector Stanley Hopkins, a detective that Holmes has great hopes for, comes to Holmes for help with the murder of Captain 'Black' Peter Carey. Carey has been found dead in his private den with a harpoon thrust through his chest which has pinned him to the wall. Hopkins can find no clue to the murderer and is not helped by the fact that no one seems sorry the Carey is dead.

Notes: This story certainly provides us with one of the more gruesome deaths in the canon. It could be a reason why the story has rarely been filmed.

Dakin wonders why Holmes states at the end of the story that he and Watson will be in Norway if needed. Perhaps the simplest answer would be a holiday. The alternative is another case that Conan Doyle simply decided never to write. There are plenty of other instances in the canon where cases are referred to that were never written.

Dakin also questions the idea that Holmes's bedroom at 221b could adjoin the sitting room. Specifically he states that the idea of a door connecting Holmes's bedroom to the sitting room is '...improbable enough...' From this it must be concluded that Mr Dakin was not so fortunate as to pay a visit to some of the houses on Baker Street to verify his conclusion.

The Sherlock Holmes Museum in Baker Street clearly demonstrates that Holmes's bedroom could adjoin the sitting room. The building shows two doors leading from the bedroom identified as Holmes's. One of these opens onto the landing and the other into the sitting room. Of course the house that the museum occupies is not the real 221b as the address did not exist at the time. However, if you assume it is representative of the other houses in the street at the time it proves that Conan Doyle's description is perfectly possible.

The Adventure of Charles Augustus Milverton

Published: April 1904
Set in: 1899
Client: Lady Eva Blackwell

Synopsis: Lady Eva Blackwell engages Holmes to act as her agent with Charles Augustus Milverton who has obtained some compromising letters she wrote when she was younger. If the contents of the letters were to be revealed they would almost certainly bring about the cancellation of her forthcoming wedding and ruin her reputation.

Holmes meets Milverton but they fail to reach an agreement and therefore Holmes decides that he needs to get into Milverton's house in order to understand the layout with a view to then burgling the house to retrieve the letters. However Holmes is not the only person pursuing Milverton.

Notes: The most outstanding fact about this story is that it is one where Holmes actually becomes engaged to be married. His fiancée is the housemaid at Milverton's house. In his guise as a plumber, Holmes becomes involved with her in order to find out the comings and goings of the house. Watson is more than a little disturbed when Holmes admits the engagement to him but Holmes assures him that there is another man who will step in once he has vanished from the scene. The whole exercise shows an element of hypocrisy on Holmes's part as when he eventually abandons the housemaid he is effectively committing breach of promise. This is the very same offence that he threatened to thrash James Windibank for in *A Case of*

Identity. Of course Holmes's ultimate aim is far nobler but the offence is still the same.

As with *The Abbey Grange* and some other cases, the decision to publish the account would have put Holmes and Watson very much within the reach of the law. Watson does state that he has depicted the case in such a way 'as to injure no one' but it would be extremely unlikely that no one would understand the real events that he was describing.

The Adventure of the Six Napoleons

Published: May 1904
Set in: 1900
Client: Scotland Yard

Synopsis: The Black Pearl of the Borgias has been stolen. Although briefly consulted on the case, Holmes did not progress far. Some time later a bizarre series of thefts occurs where the owners of a bust of Napoleon wake to find it removed and smashed nearby. Inspector Lestrade treats it as a separate case but Holmes becomes convinced that they are linked when a member of the mafia is found dead at the scene of one of the thefts.

Notes: There is a similarity between this story and *The Blue Carbuncle* in that both stories are concerned with a valuable stolen item that has been kept from the authorities by being hidden inside another object which then goes missing.

Dakin sets the date at 1900 which is based on the day that Beppo must have received his wages. Refer to his book for a deeper explanation of this. As he remarks, Lestrade's admiration for Holmes in this story certainly dates it after the events of *The Norwood Builder* in which he was more hostile.

Once again we have a reference to a case that was unfortunately never written up. Holmes refers to the '...dreadful business of the Abernetty family...' and how it was brought to his attention by how far parsley had suck into butter on a hot day. Needless to say, there has been speculation as to what this case could have been about. However all theories are destined to remain no more than that as there are no further details within this story or any other.

The truly bizarre aspect of this story is its ending. Having demonstrated to Lestrade and Watson that the missing pearl is indeed in the bust, Holmes asks Watson to put it in the safe and Lestrade is dismissed. One has to wonder why Lestrade made no attempt to take charge of the pearl. What happened to it afterwards? Is it possible that it remained in the safe perhaps along with the Blue Carbuncle? In both cases the return to the owner is not mentioned.

The Adventure of the Three Students

Published: June 1904
Set in: 1895
Client: Mr Hilton Soames

Synopsis: Holmes and Watson, who are on holiday in one of our university towns, are called in to investigate a case of possible cheating for an important Greek exam. Only three students could have examined the paper in advance. Holmes must discover who the culprit is.

Notes: Firstly we must start with the fact that there is little argument about the date which all, apart from Baring-Gould, accept is 1895. After this the differences of opinion begin to show.

The hotly debated question concerns the university. Is it Oxford or is it Cambridge? Most sources finally come down on Oxford as being the university in this case. The first argument is a reference to a quadrangle which is not a term used in Cambridge. The second is the fact that Holmes appears well acquainted with the local area and the college tutor. In *The Missing Three-Quarter*, which is set in Cambridge, Holmes is unfamiliar with the area.

As an aside we can look at the issue of Holmes's own education. At the time, the only two acceptable universities for a man of Holmes's position would have been Oxford and Cambridge. Which did he go to? Dakin is very much in favour of Oxford largely on the grounds of his familiarity with it, as just discussed. The present author is inclined to agree with this conclusion. However T.S. Blakeney comes down strongly in favour of Cambridge on the grounds that Holmes's friend and fellow undergraduate Trevor (from *The 'Gloria Scott')* was from Norfolk and likely to go to the university nearest to his home. He also suggests that if Holmes studied chemistry, he was more likely to do so at Cambridge. However these two arguments are hardly formidable. Trevor may have deliberately gone to Oxford to put as much distance between himself and his family as possible. Many a present-day undergraduate will have done the same. As for chemistry being a more likely pursuit at Cambridge, it is stated, according to the University of Oxford's official website, that Oxford had a dedicated chemistry laboratory as early as 1860 which was extended in 1878. In other words it was present and available at the time Holmes would have attended university.

The Adventure of the Golden Pince-Nez

Published: July 1904
Set in: 1894
Client: Inspector Hopkins

Synopsis: Willoughby Smith, the secretary of Professor Coram, is found dying by a maid at the professor's house. His dying words suggest that his killer is a woman but no trace of her can be found. In his hand is found a pair of golden pince-nez.

Notes: Unusually there is little disagreement about the date in which this story is set. Watson states in the first sentence that it is 1894. For a change many people have taken this as read.

Inspector Hopkins remarks that Smith was a young man '...straight from the university' and he then clarifies this by mentioning Cambridge. It is interesting to contrast the clear naming of the university in this story with the ambiguous references to universities in other stories. Was Conan Doyle intentionally keeping us in the dark as to which university Holmes went to, if so, for what purpose?

The closing part of the story raises some questions. After emerging from her hiding place, Anna states that Coram is in fact Russian but she will not reveal his true name. She then immediately uses it in the next sentence. Admittedly she only reveals his first name but to a man like Holmes it is certain that working out his full identity would not have been difficult. However we need to ask what the purpose of this secrecy was? The papers that she stole from the desk presumably contained Coram's full name if they were to be sufficient to secure the release of her friend Alexis by allocating blame to where it really belonged. She continually refers to the papers in her closing statement but she also makes a reference to her day-to-day diary. It is not clear whether or not this was also found in the desk but it would seem likely that it would have been. Furthermore one has to ask whether these papers would have really secured the release of Alexis. He was clearly considered to be dangerous by the authorities. The papers may have proved him innocent of violence but he would have almost certainly still been regarded as a subversive. Therefore his freedom was unlikely to be secured purely by the papers. Anna would have done Alexis a greater service by staying alive in order to speak as a witness on his behalf. As it was she left the case purely in the hands of Holmes who was not present at any of the events that led to Alexis' imprisonment and would therefore be of little use as a witness. Coram would not have put the noose round his own neck so it is likely that the best Alexis could have hoped for was a change in punishment rather than an end to it.

The Adventure of the Missing Three-Quarter

Published: August 1904
Set in: 1896
Client: Cyril Overton

Synopsis: Godfrey Staunton, the right wing three-quarter for the Cambridge University Rugby team, has vanished. An important match against Oxford is to take place the following day. His friend Cyril Overton comes to Holmes to beg for assistance in finding him.

Notes: Events are clearly set in Cambridge due to the address on Overton's visiting card. This story provides the most ammunition against the idea that Holmes was a student at Cambridge rather than Oxford. During the story he is clearly unfamiliar with the area and he refers to Cambridge as '...this inhospitable town...' These are hardly the words of a former student. We know that Holmes spent two years at College. It is beyond common sense to suggest that he would have such a low opinion of the place and be so ignorant of the locality after so long a period of time.

Unusually neither Dakin nor Klinger make any attempt to identify the location of Bentley's Private hotel at which the Cambridge team were staying when Staunton vanished. However the task is hardly an easy one and perhaps this is the reason. The only hotel with a similar name is situated in Harrington Gardens in Kensington. However there is no way that it can be the hotel in question as the building was built in 1880 and originally housed four private residences. There is little chance that it changed from private residences to a hotel in as little as sixteen years. However this is not the only objection to it. When Staunton runs from the hotel he is seen by the porter running down the street towards the Strand. Assuming the porter did not leave the front of the hotel and follow him it makes it clearly impossible for the hotel to be in Kensington. According to Klinger, the original manuscript has Staunton running down Northumberland Avenue towards the Embankment. This is interesting as it raises questions about Staunton's motives. Presumably, given the nature of the note, he was keen to get to Kings Cross station in order to travel to Cambridge. Therefore it hardly seems logical to head in the opposite direction to the Embankment. Perhaps this is why it was changed to the Strand for publication. This would make more sense as Staunton would have been likely to head for Trafalgar Square via the Strand in order to get a bus or cab towards Kings Cross.

Dr Leslie Armstrong is a refreshingly formidable opponent for Holmes and Holmes himself recognises it with the remark that he is worthy to fill the shoes of Professor Moriarty. He successfully manages to visit Staunton on several occasions without Holmes being able to trace his route. Holmes has to resort to a draghound and aniseed in order to confound Armstrong and discover Staunton's hiding place. Klinger informs us of the theory proposed by Marshall Berdan that Holmes was deliberately careless about tracking Armstrong until after the rugby match had been played perhaps wishing Oxford to win. He also suggests that Holmes did not consider the case urgent. This hardly seems likely given that he had read the impression of Staunton's note which said 'Stand by us for God's sake!'

The Adventure of the Abbey Grange

Published: September 1904
Set in: 1897
Client: Inspector Stanley Hopkins

Synopsis: The master of the Abbey Grange, Sir Eustace Brackenstall, is found dead, his head smashed in with a poker. His wife is found tied up and bruised in the same room. She states that a well known gang of burglars are responsible but Holmes is not so sure.

Notes: We remarked earlier, in our look at the character of Inspector Lestrade, that people were at the risk of exposure by the publication of Watson's accounts. In this case the publication would affect a number of people including Holmes and Watson themselves and put them in danger of criminal proceedings.

The criminal proceedings in question were hardly insignificant. As soon as Watson's account appeared there would have been enough evidence to have Captain Croker tried for the murder of Sir Eustace. Lady Brackenstall and her maid would be prosecuted for being accessories and for perverting the course of justice by falsely implicating innocent parties for the murder (the fact that said parties were career burglars is hardly relevant). Finally Holmes and Watson would be prosecuted for taking the law into their own hands and pardoning Croker and all concerned. Additionally it should not be forgotten that Inspector Hopkins would have been upset and angry about being deceived by Holmes. He may have been in awe of Holmes in the fashion of a pupil to master but it is hard to see how this level of respect could survive so large a deception. Dakin's remark that Croker and Lady Brackenstall may have died immediately prior to the publication does nothing to save Holmes, Watson, the maid or Hopkins so it will not stand up as a theory.

The Adventure of the Second Stain

Published: December 1904
Set in: 1894
Client: The British Government

Synopsis: An important diplomatic document goes missing from the Department for European Affairs. Its publication could lead to war. The Government hires Holmes to discover its fate and to retrieve it if possible. Holmes's initial chief suspect for the theft is murdered the next day. Is it a coincidence or are the events linked?

Notes: Some of the reasons for the confusion about the year in which this story is set have been outlined earlier (refer to The Naval Treaty). However the placing of the story in 1894 by two chronologies merits further inspection.

When Conan Doyle first mentioned this case in the opening lines of *The Naval Treaty* it was never his intention to write it as he already knew that he was going to kill Holmes at the end of the series of stories known as *The Memoirs of Sherlock Holmes*. At the time this story stood as much chance of being written as *The Tired Captain*. Other authors have suggested that more than one case may have merited the title and that Watson was referring to a different case within his account of *The Naval Treaty*. While certainly plausible it is more likely that Conan Doyle decided to use the title without worrying too much about making it fit properly with its previous outing.

Going back to the earlier remark about authors struggling to assign clearly fictional names to real people, we have another example here. Dakin states that Lord Bellinger must be William

Gladstone. He bases this largely on Watson's description of him and the illustrations that appeared in the *Strand*. However, as we have said before, does it have to be a real person? As with the King of Bohemia is it not possible that a fictional premier was created to avoid causing embarrassment to any individual or political party. The problem with the Gladstone theory is that it gives Watson very little credit for his imagination. If he was really going to the trouble to disguise Gladstone would he have given a physical description that so closely matched him?

Regardless of all this speculation, Bellinger is certainly an interesting character. He seems remarkably understanding of Hope's loss of the letter. When the letter is subsequently 'found' in Hope's despatch box Bellinger says 'Hope, I congratulate you.' One has to wonder what Hope is being congratulated for. If Bellinger had truly believed Holmes's explanation he would have had no reason to congratulate Hope for a few days of total panic and the fear of a possible war. However, his questioning of Holmes in Hope's absence during which he remarks that there '...is more in this than meets the eye.' clearly shows that he did not really accept the explanation as given. It is conceivable that he may well have suspected Lady Hilda's involvement. It would have been more sensible if Holmes were to have obtained the letter from Lady Hilda and then taken it away with him and returned it later to Bellinger having thought up some plausible explanation for its absence in the meantime.

His Last Bow

Contains nine stories published 1908–1913 and 1917. There are only seven titles listed as two of the two-part stories were later merged under two titles rather than four. Various illustrators were brought in following the death of Sidney Paget. His brother Walter, who was supposed to have received the original commission, produced four illustrations for *The Adventure of the Dying Detective.*

The quality of the stories since Holmes was resurrected is frequently debated. Those contained within *His Last Bow* and *The Casebook of Sherlock Holmes* come in for more criticism than most. Those who 'play the game' have a variety of reasons for this that range from Watson's poor memory (again) to a mysterious editor that supposedly constructed accounts from Watson's incomplete notes. Interesting as these theories are (and we shall explore some of them later) they are easily dismissed if you look at Conan Doyle's correspondence with his mother as detailed in *Arthur Conan Doyle – A life in Letters.*

In April 1908 Conan Doyle wrote to his mother about the recent completion of a Holmes story and his plans for future ones. He went on to state that they would not hurt his reputation and that the money would be 'useful'. This reveals two facts. Firstly that he knew he was writing material that was inferior to his earlier efforts and, secondly, that it was more or less purely for financial gain.

The Adventure of Wisteria Lodge

Published: September 1908 – October 1908
Set in: 1895
Client: Mr John Scott Eccles

Synopsis: Eccles makes the acquaintance of man called Garcia through a mutual friend. Garcia later invites him to visit him at his home. When he awakes the next day he finds the house totally empty and engages Holmes to discover the reason for such a bad joke. Garcia is subsequently found dead some distance from the house with his head smashed in with a large blunt instrument.

Notes: This case is the other in which there are two police inspectors involved. In this case they are Inspector Gregson of Scotland Yard and Inspector Baynes of the Surrey police. However Gregson's involvement pretty much begins and ends at the start of the story as he is used by Baynes when he is forced to come onto Scotland Yard's territory in order to pursue Scott Eccles. After the action relocates to Surrey Gregson has no further involvement.

One of the biggest problems with this case is the date. Watson states that the events take place in March 1892 but the totally insurmountable problem with this is that it is during the period when Holmes was presumed dead. So does the case date from before Holmes's disappearance or after his return? The arguments are all in favour of the latter. *The Norwood Builder*, which most agree is set in 1894, contains a reference to an ex-President Murillo and this must surely be the Murillo concerned in this case. The same argument is made by Dakin and it seems the most sensible. The date stated above of 1895, which comes from Klinger's chronology, therefore must be wrong as Klinger agrees that *The Norwood Builder* takes place in 1894. The only way you can get around this would be to suggest that the case concerning Murillo's papers was a different (and earlier) case to the one at Wisteria Lodge. However, if Holmes had been involved with Murillo before he would surely have known precisely where he was living and the Wisteria Lodge mystery would not have been so dark to him at the beginning.

So what inferences can we draw from all this? You could suggest that the two Murillo cases concerned different people but the idea that there were two President Murillos is rather far fetched. If you assume that the two cases concern the same man then you must either take the line that Holmes knew a lot more about Wisteria Lodge than he let on or that Conan Doyle had made another mistake.

The final word on this story has to be reserved for Inspector Baynes. He is clearly the only official figure to come anywhere close to Holmes in intelligence and intuition. Holmes himself compliments Baynes more than once on his abilities. However this level of intelligence was also Baynes' downfall as a character. As remarked before, it was simply not possible for Conan Doyle to have any characters that were close to Holmes's own level on a regular basis. It is for this same reason that Mycroft and Moriarty feature in only two stories.

The Adventure of the Bruce-Partington Plans

Published: December 1908
Set in: 1895
Client: The British Government

Synopsis: Arthur Cadogan West is found dead by the side of the Metropolitan Line with a major head injury. In his pockets are found some of the plans for the Bruce-Partington submarine, a top-secret navy project. Holmes is called in, at the request of his brother Mycroft, to locate the missing plans but also ends up investigating the cause of West's death due to his suspicion at the official explanation of its cause.

Notes: When looking at the character of Watson earlier we saw how his attitude to breaking the law varied. As discussed, Holmes called on Watson's help to get into someone else's house on three occasions (*A Scandal in Bohemia, Charles Augustus Milverton* and this story). In each case the intention was to either locate or remove one or more items. Only in this story does Watson show distaste for the idea.

This gives us yet another problem of inconsistency. The main problem occurs with the latter two cases of the three. According to the chronologies of both Dakin and Klinger the Milverton case is set in 1899 with *The Bruce-Partington Plans* set in 1895. However they were published in the opposite order with the Milverton story appearing in 1904 as opposed to 1908 for *The Bruce-Partington Plans*. If you present the three stories in the accepted chronological order Watson goes from being happy at breaking the law, in *A Scandal in Bohemia,* to being uncomfortable doing so before returning to being comfortable again. It is an anomaly but not an especially serious one. Predictably Baring-Gould removes this anomaly by allocating some of Holmes's lines to Watson. In his version of events Watson does not even hesitate.

Blakeney informs us of another interesting inconsistency. He draws our attention to Holmes's varying knowledge of the world of espionage. In this case Holmes specifically requests that Mycroft provide him with a list of spies resident in the country who would be interested in the plans. However, in *The Adventure of the Second Stain*, which takes place before this case, he is well aware of the international spies who would be interested in the potentially explosive letter that he has been tasked with recovering. It is certainly an anomaly but not an impossible one. There must have been new foreign agents within Great Britain by the time of the theft of the Bruce-Partington plans. Hence Holmes's request to Mycroft can be easily explained as the need for an update to his existing knowledge. The knowledge he had of spies during *The Second Stain* was almost certainly gained from Mycroft, in much the same fashion, on some prior occasion.

At the beginning of this case, Mycroft informs Holmes that a successful outcome could result in an honour. Holmes makes it clear that he has no interest in receiving one. Most fans will know that mention is made of Holmes refusing a Knighthood in *The Three Garridebs*. Was the offer to Knight Holmes due to his services in this case? We shall look at this again in our examination of *The Three Garridebs*.

The Adventure of the Devil's Foot

Published: December 1910
Set in: 1897
Client: Reverend Roundhay

Synopsis: Three members of the Tregennis family are found, in the dining room of their house, by their housekeeper. The two brothers are mad and their sister is dead. Local rumour has it that the devil was involved. Reverend Roundhay and the last brother, Mortimer, bring in Holmes, who is on convalescence in the area, to investigate. Holmes is suspicious of Mortimer's description of the events leading up to the discovery of his siblings. However he is unable to question Mortimer further as he is subsequently found dead in similar circumstances.

Notes: Watson is clear about the date being 1897 and none of the usual authorities disagree with this.

Holmes and Watson find themselves in Cornwall due to the need for Holmes to rest. This is quite interesting in itself. According to Watson a Dr Moore Agar of Harley Street had ordered Holmes to rest. Clearly Dr Agar was some kind of specialist as Holmes was sure to turn to Watson for day-to-day medical issues. This begs the question of what exactly was wrong with Holmes. The text infers drug use but this would seem unlikely. Watson states that Holmes had been working excessively hard and that this had led to his health faltering. As he turned to drugs only in times of boredom it would seem unlikely for them to be at the root of his problems on this occasion. It is more likely that Holmes's practice of not eating for days at a time during a case led to his ill health. Watson goes on to say that only the threat of being '…permanently disqualified from work' induced Holmes to take some rest.

How exactly was such a threat made? The only plausible option would have been the threat to confine Holmes to some kind of asylum or other medical institution. Both he and Watson would have been aware that such an event would have damaged his career as by this time accounts of his cases had already appeared and he would have been a known figure. As such his confinement would have been newsworthy and widely reported. It would seem likely therefore that some kind of compromise was struck whereby Watson would accompany Holmes to Cornwall to ensure that he took his rest.

Holmes's ultimate decision to allow Dr Sterndale to go to Africa instead of making him face up to his crime is consistent with his attitude towards previous characters in similar positions. Dakin takes issues with Holmes's remark that he might have acted the same as Sterndale had he been in a similar situation. This is another case of putting Holmes on a moral pedestal. There was no suggestion by Holmes that he would act in exactly the same way he was simply suggesting that under similar circumstances he might kill for vengeance. In *The Adventure of the Speckled Band* he admitted to being indirectly responsible for causing the death of Dr Roylott so this vengeful sentiment is not as out of character as some have suggested.

The surviving Tregennis brothers were sent to Helston. This refers to the workhouse which was situated in the town of the same name. Records from 1867 showed that few of its inmates were suffering from mental problems. Of all the inmates of that time only seven were considered as 'insane' or 'idiotic'. Approximately forty miles away in Bodmin there was an official lunatic asylum to which it seems probable the brothers were eventually conveyed.

The Adventure of the Red Circle

Published: March 1911 – April 1911
Set in: 1902
Client: Mrs Warren

Synopsis: Mrs Warren comes to Holmes for advice when one of her tenants refuses to leave their room and starts to communicate entirely by written notes.

Notes: There is considerable confusion over the date of this story. According to various sources the date could lie almost anywhere between 1895 and 1902. According to Dakin, Rolfe Boswell stated that the date must be after 1901 due to Holmes's reference to one of the tenant's notes to Mrs Warren having a part removed, possibly to conceal a thumbprint. As mentioned in the discussion of *The Norwood Builder*, fingerprint identification was adopted by Scotland Yard in 1901 so this fits chronologically. However why would the tenant be so eager to hide a thumbprint? Signora Lucca (the tenant) was not in fear of the police and had committed no crime in England which would have resulted in her prints being taken. It is not likely that the Red Circle society kept fingerprint records so it is doubtful that she feared such identification. If the mark in question were indeed a thumbprint she was probably more concerned that it would reveal her gender and show that she was not the original tenant. It was for the same reason that the notes to Mrs Warren were printed. Thus we have removed one of the arguments for a post 1901 date. However, as there are no convincing theories for any date, we shall leave the date as 1902 in accordance with the chronologies of Klinger and Baring-Gould.

Dakin questions why Gennaro should send messages to Emilia in English rather than their native Italian tongue. It is a reasonable question but a possible answer lies in their conduct throughout the story. Regardless of logic they went out of their way at all times to draw as little attention to their actions as possible. Perhaps they reasoned that messages in an English paper that were written in Italian would stand out. Therefore the decision was made to write them in English in order to effectively hide their message in plain sight.

Dakin also questions why they should use a newspaper at all when a simple letter would have sufficed. There is a possible explanation for this also. A single letter could easily go astray whereas placing the message in a newspaper ensured thousands of copies being printed and virtually no chance of the message not being received.

The Disappearance of Lady Frances Carfax

Published: December 1911
Set in: 1901
Client: The Carfax family

Synopsis: Lady Frances vanishes soon after making the acquaintance of a Major Shlessinger at a hotel in Baden. Holmes despatches Watson to investigate on his behalf. Does her disappearance have anything to do with the mysterious man who has been trailing her?

Notes: Once again we have significant disagreement about the date. Klinger, as we can see, places events in 1901 but he accepts that there is no consensus about the date he has chosen. The only aspect, about which we can be certain, according to Dakin, is that the events are after 1889 as this is when Dr Shlessinger's (alias Holy Peters) ear was bitten during a fight. Dakin goes further to suggest that, as Holmes refers to the fight as taking place in 1889, the year must have been at least 1891 as Holmes would have referred to it as last year if it had been 1890. He also draws our attention to the theory of a Dr Theodore Gibson who states that the events must have taken place before 1898 which is a time when we know Holmes to have a telephone installed. The assumption behind this is that when Holmes realised that the plan was to bury Lady Frances alive it would have made more sense to telephone for assistance that could have made it to her location quicker than he and Watson could have managed in a cab. The fact that he did not is taken as indicative of the date being prior to 1898. This is a strong argument but is not impossible to overcome. It could be seen as tenuous but there is always the possibility that Holmes's telephone could have been out of order and therefore unavailable for use. Regrettably therefore the date is destined to remain elusive.

The Adventure of the Dying Detective

Published: December 1913
Set in: 1890
Client: None

Synopsis: Watson comes to Baker Street to find Holmes suffering from a serious illness. Despite his evident condition Holmes refuses to let Watson treat him. Instead he insists that Watson fetches Culverton Smith, an expert on tropical diseases.

Notes: There is little argument about the date. Watson refers to the case taking place in the second year of his married life. This places it in 1890 as he undoubtedly married in 1888 after events of *The Sign of Four*.

Watson's reference to his married life is in itself interesting. It is of course open to interpretation (like all Sherlockian theories are) but this remark does seem to suggest that this marriage is Watson's first. It is purely a personal opinion but it sounds like the kind of remark to come from someone new to the state of marriage rather than someone who had been married before.

Dakin highlights what he sees as an inconsistency between this story and *The Illustrious Client*. In this story Holmes deceives Watson about his health in order to make him seem more convincing when he goes to Culverton Smith for aid. In *The Illustrious Client* Holmes gets Watson to exaggerate his injuries and relies on his ability to 'put it on thick' for the press. Dakin states that this happened 'A few years later' and hence his belief that it demonstrates an inconsistency regarding Holmes's belief in Watson's ability to lie convincingly. However, Dakin's very own chronology puts the events of *The*

Illustrious Client in 1902 a full twelve years after the events of this story. This is hardly 'A few years later'. Is it not possible to infer that, in just over a decade, Watson's abilities at dissimulation had improved?

His Last Bow

Published: September 1917
Set in: 1914
Client: British Government

Synopsis: Von Bork, a German agent, is waiting for his best agent to bring him some papers regarding British naval signals before he leaves England for Germany. The agent in question is Altamont, an Irish-American from Chicago.

Notes: Chronologically this is the last documented case that Holmes works on. It is also told in the third-person, the first occasion that Conan Doyle was to write a story that was not from the perspective of Watson.

The date, at least, is beyond doubt and is August 1914. This is just as well as there are plenty of other anomalies to occupy us when looking at this story. We begin with Holmes's reference to Irene Adler. When explaining his true identity to Von Bork he states that he was involved in the separation of Miss Adler from the late King of Bohemia. Looked at one way, this suggests that they actually desired to be together and that Holmes prevented it. This is, of course, is patently false. The King wanted no more than to be away from Adler. So we are left with only two interpretations. The first, and most likely, is that this was another of Conan Doyle's mistakes. The second, albeit tenuous, is that the 'separation' refers to Holmes's success in removing Irene Adler's influence from the King's life (by scaring her off) and thus preventing any scandal involving the compromising photograph.

We then have to return to the manner in which the story is written. Of course it cannot be written from Watson's perspective as he was not present for the first two-thirds of the events as depicted. Many theories have sprung up in an attempt to deal with this. The problem lies with the fact that no one person was witness to all the events described in the story. Dakin determines that the story is by Watson but written in the third-person to get around the fact that there were parts in which he was not directly involved. You can accept this up to a point. Watson can obviously write about the events following the 'arrest' of Von Bork but how do we account for the other parts of the story?

Holmes could obviously have related the parts in which he was involved to Watson later but exactly when would he have done this? The story makes it quite clear that all the conversation between Holmes and Watson was about 'the days of the past' and, in any case, they only spoke 'for a few minutes'. This was hardly enough time for Watson to make a note of all of the conversation that passed between Holmes and Von Bork. Dakin's idea that Holmes would have filled Watson in afterwards is cast into some doubt by the short time that they had together in private coupled with Holmes's prediction that the chat on the terrace would be the 'last quiet talk' that they were likely to have. In addition we have to examine the parts of the story where both Holmes and Watson were not present such as the conversations between Von Bork and Baron Von Herling. As Dakin points out, the maid Martha must have spent a lot of time with her ear to the keyhole in order to hear all that passed between them. Dakin's attempt to get round this takes the form that Watson exercised his imagination to fill in gaps in his tale. All this serves to illustrate is the desperate situation you get yourself into if you insist on behaving as if it were all true.

Finally we must ask ourselves why Holmes was convinced that his conversation with Watson might be their last. The clear suggestion in the story is that Watson has volunteered his services to the inevitable war effort, most likely to a home based hospital for invalided soldiers as he was clearly too old for foreign deployment. If you accept the chronologies as laid down by Dakin and Baring-Gould, Holmes was sixty and Watson sixty-two at the time of this story. They were hardly two men on the brink of death so what lay behind Holmes's remark? You could of course theorise that Holmes was seriously ill, knew he was close to death and chose to keep it from Watson. It would of course not be the first time that he had kept Watson in the dark. Conan Doyle provides no clues here. The only argument against this theory comes from Baring-Gould who suggests that Holmes was not to die until 1957.

The Valley of Fear

Published: September 1914 – May 1915
Set in: 1888
Client: Inspector MacDonald

Synopsis: Holmes receives two letters from Porlock, an informer from within Professor Moriarty's organisation. The first is in code and the second letter requests that he destroys the first. Holmes deciphers the original letter to discover a warning that a man named Douglas of Birlstone House is in danger. Shortly afterwards Inspector MacDonald arrives to tell them that Douglas was murdered the previous night.

Notes: This is the last of the four novels and was published after *The Dying Detective* and before *His Last Bow*.

It opens with the discussion between Holmes and Watson about Moriarty. The issues with this have already been touched upon in our look at *The Final Problem* and shall not be revisited here. This story raises plenty of other interesting questions with which we can occupy ourselves. The first questions concern Porlock himself. According to Holmes, Porlock has been a long-standing informer. You cannot help but wonder how Porlock managed to get away with informing on Moriarty if the latter was supposed to be such a genius. When Holmes and Moriarty have their interview at the beginning of *The Final Problem*, Moriarty lists the occasions that Holmes had frustrated him. We can assume that Porlock's informing skills were behind at least some of Holmes's successes so it is odd that Moriarty never thought to look among his own ranks for the cause of his problems. Of course, the other way to interpret this is to assume that Moriarty was aware of Porlock's treachery and used it for his own ends or that the two of them collaborated to give Holmes leads on certain cases as a way of distracting him from other more important ones. An undeniable fact is that not all Holmes's cases were successes. At the opening of *The Problem of Thor Bridge* Watson makes it clear that some of the cases he has records of were 'complete failures'. Who is to say that some of these failures were not masterminded by Moriarty? It is only our natural desire to dwell on our hero's successes that prevents us from believing that Moriarty or others could occasionally frustrate him.

Staying with Moriarty, at the time of this story he is still a serving professor and Inspector MacDonald actually relates to Holmes and Watson the story of a visit he made to see him. We know from *The Final Problem* that Moriarty was forced to resign his university chair due to some scandal yet there are only three years between the stories if you accept the chronologies put forward by Klinger, Dakin and Baring-Gould who all put *The Valley of Fear* in 1888 and *The Final Problem* in 1891.

If the scandal had already broken in 1891 it follows that it must have occurred soon after 1888 perhaps between then and 1890. One idea as to what this scandal could have been is made very early on in this story. Holmes remarks to Inspector MacDonald about a painting hanging in Moriarty's study by the artist Jean-Baptiste Greuze, a French artist who lived from 1725 to 1805. This painting, entitled *La Jeune Fille a l'Agneau*, was worth forty thousand pounds and Moriarty was earning only seven hundred pounds a year from his university. It is possible that after the events of this story Inspector MacDonald began enquiries about the purchase that led to Moriarty having to give up his position. This is not stated in *The Final Problem* probably because Conan Doyle had no specific scandal in mind as he had no plans for further stories at that time and there was therefore no need to worry about such loose ends.

Taking another look at Moriarty's organisation, Holmes reveals that Moriarty pays Colonel Sebastian Moran a salary of six thousand pounds a year and that this was more than the Prime Minister received. According to the House of Commons Information Office Fact sheet on Ministerial Salaries, in 1831 the salary for the office of Prime Minister (or First Lord of the Treasury) was five thousand pounds. In 1930 the salary was unchanged. So if we assume that the salary did not change for one hundred years then the Prime Minster of the time (in 1888, the Marquess of Salisbury) would have been earning one thousand pounds less that Colonel Moran. This is indicative of the sheer amount of ill gotten money flowing into Moriarty's crime network.

The Case-Book of Sherlock Holmes

Contains twelve stories published 1921–1927. Conan Doyle was to die three years after the last story was published.

Sherlockian authors seem to have more problems with this series of stories than any other. This is largely due to the fact that this series contains three of the four stories which were not written from the perspective of Watson. We shall examine some of the problems with these particular stories later.

The stories collected under the titles of *The Adventures of Sherlock Holmes, The Memoirs of Sherlock Holmes* and *The Return of Sherlock Holmes* were all published at the rate of one per month. From the series *His Last Bow* onwards the elapsed time between the publication dates of the individual stories starts to lengthen. It is not unreasonable to put this down to three influencing factors - Conan Doyle's increasing dislike of the Holmes stories, his equally increasing interest in spiritualism and, finally, his non-Holmes novels. Many authors have remarked that the quality of the stories was never the same after *The Final Problem*. Such remarks led to the bizarre suggestion by Anthony Boucher in his essay - *Was the later Holmes an Impostor?* - that Holmes did in fact die and was secretly replaced by his cousin Sherrinford. The name Sherrinford was the name that Conan Doyle had originally intended to use before he came up with the name of Sherlock. Apparently, according to the theory, Sherrinford's lesser powers were the reason for the drop in the quality of the cases.

However, the reduced pace of output and quality can be more easily ascribed to the fact that Conan Doyle was writing the stories for the money rather than enjoyment. The stories collected under the title of *His Last Bow* were published between September 1908 and September 1917, a much longer period than with the previous three series. There was, of course, a break in the middle of these adventures when Conan Doyle wrote his last Holmes novel *The Valley of Fear* and published it in parts between September 1914 and May 1915. Another reason for the delay betweens the stories in *His Last Bow* would be that Conan Doyle was working on his other famous novels *The Lost World,* which was to be published in 1912, and *The Poison Belt,* published in 1913. These stories were the first two featuring his other famous creation - Professor Challenger.

Similarly large gaps in publication occur in *The Casebook of Sherlock Holmes* - where the stories were published between October 1921 and February 1927. These gaps were mostly caused by Conan Doyle's written output devoted to spiritualism. Between 1921 and 1927 Conan Doyle produced no less than five works on the subject beginning with *The Wanderings of a Spiritualist* in 1921 and ending with *The History of Spiritualism* in 1926. It is not unreasonable to suggest that the reduction in the quality of the later Holmes cases was more down to a combination of Conan Doyle's lack of interest in Holmes and the distraction of working on his many other publications. The story *The Lion's Mane,* which Dakin is dismissive of largely due to Holmes's uncharacteristic language, was published in 1926 around the same time as *The History of Spiritualism.* Conan Doyle was almost certainly working on the two in parallel and each could have easily impacted upon the other.

T.S. Blakeney, in his essay *Sherlock Holmes: Fact or Fiction?,* suggests that all of the stories making up *His Last Bow* and *The Casebook of Sherlock Holmes* are in fact genuine accounts but that they have been altered or touched-up by a mysterious editor. With the *Casebook* in particular this is given as the main reason for the inferior quality of the writing, the accounts written in the third-person (supposedly from Watson's rough notes) and the uncharacteristic lines attributed to Holmes, which have offended the sensibilities of many a Sherlockian author. However we must not forget the letter of April 1908, to which we have already referred, in which Conan Doyle admitted that his later stories were inferior and that he clearly was not concerned about it.

The Adventure of the Mazarin Stone

Published: October 1921
Set in: 1903
Client: The British Government

Synopsis: The Mazarin Stone has been stolen. Holmes has been called in to investigate and has determined that Count Sylvius is the thief. However, although he has some evidence, he does not know where the stone is. When Sylvius decides to visit him at Baker Street, Holmes attempts to extract the stone's location from him.

Notes: This story is told in the third-person which makes it unusual and only the second story to be written in such a fashion after *His Last Bow*.

Dakin is as dismissive of this story as *The Three Gables* (see later). On this occasion his justification rests on the fact that the story is told in the third-person and therefore it cannot be either a direct recollection of Watson or a retelling by him of a case related to him by Holmes, the latter typified by the cases of *The Gloria Scott* and *The Musgrave Ritual*. Dakin goes as far as to suggest that Watson made notes on the events he was witness to and then some third-party filled in the missing sections using a heavy dose of dramatic licence. Apparently this is the reason for the remarks attributed to Holmes which Dakin considers to be unworthy.

Once again we must restate that if the stories were truly historical accounts these objections would all be valid but, as they are Conan Doyle's work, we have to accept that he was entitled to use whatever perspective he wished. If you accept the story publication order from *The Strand*, this was only the second story to be written from a non-Watson standpoint. Is it not feasible to suppose that Conan Doyle, after writing nearly all his stories up to this point from the point of view of Watson, would struggle to change to a third-person perspective in a seamless fashion?

Dakin eventually steps back from his conclusion and sticks with his first instinct which is to disregard the story entirely. In this he gives himself little choice as it would be highly unlikely that Watson, had he been a real person, would have let someone else complete his stories for him. Baring-Gould, at least, is not dismissive of the story but he gets over the manner in which it was written, in his characteristic fashion, by leaving out the vast majority of the story reducing it to the closing part only.

There is an interesting architectural anomaly with this story which Dakin picks up on. Holmes remarks that there are two doors from his bedroom into the sitting room. We have already seen from our look at *Black Peter* that it was perfectly possible for Holmes's bedroom to have a door that connected to the sitting room as well as one connecting to the landing. However the idea that there were two doors from the bedroom to the sitting room is a step too far and was clearly contrived by Conan Doyle purely for the purpose of the story's plot. It must go down as just another of those literary devices that mark the *Casebook* out as the series with the most inconsistencies.

It was clearly unusual and perhaps unwise for Conan Doyle to change from his usual style of giving us the story through the eyes of Watson. This was his second attempt at a different angle and the second occasion he was to write a story in the third-person. Perhaps he was aware of the disadvantages of this approach as his future non-Watson stories would be told from the perspective of Holmes himself.

162

The Problem of Thor Bridge

Published: February 1922 – March 1922
Set in: 1901
Client: Senator Gibson

Synopsis: The wife of a former American senator is found dead on a bridge on his English estate. The cause of death is a gunshot wound to the head. Suspicion falls on the governess when a pistol with one discharged chamber is found in her room. The former senator, who is convinced of the governess' innocence, hires Holmes to investigate.

Notes: This is the second story in the canon where the villain is dead from the beginning. The plot is ingenious and, in the author's opinion, is the best in the *Casebook* series.

Baring-Gould is of the opinion that the events of this case took place in 1900. Dakin and Klinger agree on 1901. However Dakin's reason for this date as opposed to 1900 is that he believes that *The Hound of the Baskervilles* took place in 1900 (see earlier) and therefore Watson would have been at Baskerville Hall. The date certainly has to be before 1903 as we know Watson had remarried by that time. However it cannot be 1902 as Watson describes himself as living in Queen Anne Street in that year (which will be examined in more detail later). In this story Watson is clearly resident in Baker Street as he describes himself as descending to breakfast. The obvious inference being that he had come down from his second floor bedroom to the sitting room.

Curiously other authors have very little to say upon this story and this is no doubt due to the fact that there is little about it to analyse. Dakin spends less than two pages on it and

Baring-Gould barely mentions it at all. The aspect of the story that tantalises the most is actually a number of references made by Watson regarding other cases. The case of Isadora Persano and the worm unknown to science is certainly an intriguing idea but, had it been written, there is a good chance that it could well have stretched the bounds of plausibility as much as *The Creeping Man*. The case of James Phillimore, who disappeared after going to retrieve his umbrella, had a lot more potential but it was ultimately left to other authors to provide the details.

However this story has contributed one very important line to the Sherlockian world. It features Holmes's immortal line regarding his fees. In response to Senator Gibson's promise of significant financial rewards for success Holmes states 'My professional charges are upon a fixed scale. I do not vary them, save when I remit them altogether.' This line has made it into more than one Holmes feature film. The most recent example, at the time of writing, occurred in 2004.

The Adventure of the Creeping Man

Published: March 1923
Set in: 1903
Client: Mr. Trevor Bennett & Edith Presbury

Synopsis: Professor Presbury starts to behave oddly soon after his engagement to the daughter of a colleague. He begins receiving secret correspondence and is seen moving around his house on all fours. One night, his daughter Edith wakes at night to see her father outside her window. She cannot understand how this can be as her room is two floors up and inaccessible. In fear of her safety she asks Holmes's advice.

Notes: This is arguably one of the most bizarre cases in the canon and goes against Conan Doyle's normally sound scientific principles. The idea that an injection of monkey serum would provide rejuvenation and monkey like characteristics is fantastic indeed and has no scientific basis.

The reference to Camford University which is clearly an amalgamation of Oxford and Cambridge has caused a great deal of debate. In fact the level of debate over this is second only to the debate about which university Holmes himself attended. The arguments in favour of Oxford are the strongest. Holmes's reference to the Chequers, which is clearly some kind of inn or hotel, could equally apply to Oxford or Cambridge as both boast inns of that name. However in the case of Cambridge the inns (Cambridge has more than one Chequers) in question are not in central Cambridge but on the outskirts. Holmes makes it very clear that the Chequers he refers to is in close proximity to the railway station. The Chequers in Oxford is just over half a mile from the station and is on Oxford's High

Street. If any further proof were needed it can be found in *The New Annotated Sherlock Holmes* where Klinger points out that only Oxford University had a chair of Comparative Anatomy at the time the story is set and this is the position that Presbury held.

The Adventure of the Sussex Vampire

Published: January 1924
Set in: 1896
Client: Mr Robert Ferguson

Synopsis: Holmes receives two letters, one from a solicitor and one from their client Robert Ferguson seeking his advice on vampires. He suspects that his wife has been drinking the blood of their baby son and she has assaulted his son of fifteen from his first marriage.

Notes: This story is one large tale of family dysfunction with each member having their own issues and being unable or unwilling to discuss them with the others. As such it needed the vampire connection to make it of interest or, as Holmes might say, lift it from the commonplace.

It may not be the most tactful analogy but there have been cases where the family dog has attacked a new baby because it feels its position in the household has been usurped. The scenario is mirrored here with Ferguson's older son Jack attacking the baby because he deems him to have stolen his father's affections from him. The trial-run of using his poison on the family dog is clearly reminiscent of the sheep injuries featured in *Silver Blaze*.

Dakin seizes on the use of the word 'kiddies' by Ferguson to describe his children. Once again he accuses Watson of a memory slip in using the term and questions whether it was in use in the 1890s. However, according to the *Online Entomology Dictionary,* using the term 'kid' to describe a child was very much established by the 1840s. Admittedly this source refers to usage in the United States but it is perfectly reasonable to suppose that the term had made it to England during the following fifty years.

The Adventure of the Three Garridebs

Published: January 1925
Set in: 1902
Client: Nathan Garrideb

Synopsis: Holmes is contacted by an old academic called Nathan Garrideb who wishes to enlist his help in tracing another person of the same family name. A mysterious will left by an American Garrideb split his large fortune three ways if three Garridebs could be found to claim the money. An American by the name of John Garrideb was the first and tracked down Nathan in England after finding no other Garridebs in America.

John Garrideb later visits Holmes to protest at his involvement but then softens when Holmes suggests that he may be able to help. The American's story about the Garrideb will arouses Holmes's suspicions and he is even more suspicious when the American subsequently claims to find another Garrideb without his help. When Holmes discovers that the American has convinced Nathan Garrideb to visit the mysterious third man he begins to wonder if there is something about the academic himself that the American is interested in.

Notes: Again Conan Doyle seems to have recycled the original idea used in *The Red-Headed League* and later in *The Stockbroker's Clerk*. Once more we have a man lured out of a location, where he is in the way, by the promise of large amounts of money. The other aspect that this story shares with *The Red-Headed League* is that the deception involves an eccentric America based millionaire.

For a change this story does not face any accusations about its authenticity. Dakin describes it as 'undoubtedly by Watson'. Blakeney and Baring-Gould largely skip over the story with the former devoting about one sentence to it and the latter three short paragraphs. The differing levels of importance given to the stories by authors is a subject worthy of analysis in its own right but undoubtedly falls outside the scope of this book.

It is clear, at the time of the events described, that Watson and Holmes are living together. Yet, according to the chronology, three months later, at the time of *The Illustrious Client*, Watson is living apart from Holmes in Queen Anne Street. This anomaly has been picked up by many scholars and we shall examine it in more details in the analysis of *The Illustrious Client* below.

In the opening part of the story Watson remarks that the date is easy to remember as it was in the same month that Holmes refused a knighthood for some unnamed service. The question is why should he refuse a knighthood? Holmes clearly had no aversion to honours as he had accepted the Legion of Honour in 1894 (described in *The Adventure of the Golden Pince-Nez*). Perhaps it was a nod to his French ancestry to accept the latter but why refuse the former?

The answer to the question comes from Conan Doyle's private correspondence. In 1902 rumours circulated that Conan Doyle was to be offered an honour. He was not happy at the idea of a knighthood, which he assumed would be the honour on offer. However he subsequently relented and decided that he could not refuse it without appearing rude. He remained uncomfortable about it and this no doubt manifested itself in Holmes's refusal of the same honour. Any doubt is largely dispelled by the fact that the story is set in the same year as Doyle's knighthood was awarded.

Continuing on this theme, it is interesting to speculate as to which services Holmes is supposed to have rendered to be considered for a knighthood. In *The Bruce-Partington Plans,* Mycroft suggests that a successful outcome could result in Holmes being honoured. It is therefore possible to argue that this was the case that led to the attempt to award Holmes his knighthood. However, there are a number of objections to this theory. Firstly, Holmes makes it very clear to Mycroft that he has no interest in such an honour. Secondly, *The Bruce-Partington Plans* was published thirteen years before *The Three Garridebs* so there would be no need to be so secretive about the case that led to the award. Finally, according to the chronology provided by Klinger, the stories are set seven years apart which would seem rather a long time to wait for an honour.

The Adventure of the Illustrious Client

Published: February 1925 – March 1925
Set in: 1902
Client: King Edward VII (allegedly)

Synopsis: Sir James Damery visits Holmes to ask him to find a way to prevent the marriage of Violet de Merville, a famous general's daughter, to Baron Gruner, an Austrian nobleman. Holmes is resistant when he discovers that Sir James is the agent of a client who wishes to remain anonymous and is minded to refuse. However the news that the case involves Baron Gruner keeps him interested as he is aware that Gruner has committed murder in the past and escaped the law.

Notes: As briefly noted above, at the time of these events Holmes and Watson are not living together. Watson remarks early on that he was living in his own quarters in Queen Anne Street. Some commentators have taken this to be evidence that Watson had married again. Dakin points out, quite reasonably, that if Holmes and Watson were living together only three months before during *The Three Garridebs* it does seem somewhat absurd that he should have moved out and married in so short a space of time without remarking upon it.

Dakin's explanation for the move is that Watson was back in medical practice. This is also perfectly reasonable as, at the turn of the twentieth century, Queen Anne Street had become a popular location for doctors who could not find space in Harley Street (with which it connects). The question of course is if Watson returned to practice it was presumably because he needed more money than his army pension could provide. If the reason for this need of extra money was not to support a new wife and establishment what was it? Dakin infers that Watson needed to clear debts associated with his love of horse racing. Given Watson's remark in *Shoscombe Old Place* (detailed later) about spending half his wound pension on racing you would be forgiven for being tempted to agree. However this reference to half his pension, bearing in mind the context in which it is uttered, is likely to have been an exaggeration designed to reemphasise to Holmes his knowledge of all things horse racing related and thus indicate how useful his knowledge would be in an investigation. In this he was successful as Holmes immediately made Watson his 'Handy Guide to the Turf'.

Despite his lack of reference to it we really should accept the remarriage theory as Holmes, in *The Blanched Soldier* which is set in 1903, remarks that Watson had 'deserted me for a wife'. Dakin gets over this problem by dismissing *The Blanched Soldier* as a fabricated story. He is able to do as he is working from the 'playing the game' position. If you take the opposite view, and work from the position that Conan Doyle wrote the stories, you need to accept that the marriage happened. There will be more on this marriage in the analysis of *The Blanched Soldier*.

The Adventure of the Three Gables

Published: September 1926 (The New Annotated Sherlock Holmes gives the date as October 1920 but this must be a misprint)
Set in: 1902
Client: Mrs Mary Maberley

Synopsis: Mrs Maberley has been living in her house for a little over a year when she receives a visit from a house agent who wishes to purchase the property on behalf of his mysterious client. She is astounded when told that if she agrees she will not only be selling the house but its entire contents as well, none of which she will be allowed to remove.

She calls Holmes in for advice and he becomes convinced that the events have something to do with the recent death of her son Douglas who was lately attaché in Rome.

Notes: This story shares a similarity with *The Blue Carbuncle* and *The Six Napoleons* in that it features a valuable object that is hidden inside something else.

Dakin and Blakeney agree on the year 1903 for this story on the grounds that it is clear that Watson is not living with Holmes. However we know Watson to have moved out of Baker Street in 1902 (see *The Illustrious Client*) so the events could have easily been in 1902 and Dakin does acknowledge this.

Dakin is highly dismissive of this story and suggests that it does not come from the pen of Watson at all. His reasons for this are that he considers the plot to be both fantastic and improbable. He also highlights inconsistencies in the character of Holmes.

To deal with the first point, the plot is hardly the most incredible in the series. There a plenty more unlikely plots. *The Creeping Man* is considerably less credible than this story although, in fairness, Dakin is largely dismissive of it as well. Dakin's second point regarding, what he refers to as, '...the poor figure Holmes cuts...' would be reasonable if Holmes was a real person. Once again he only serves to highlight the holes you get yourself into if you treat the characters as real people.

Despite this, it is true that Holmes is not depicted well in this story. However there are only a few remarks that he makes which could be read as racist. The others, which make reference to Steve Dixie's unpleasant body odour, could be levelled at any hired thug with perhaps less than regular access to a bath. We need to remember that Conan Doyle had been reluctantly writing Holmes stories ever since *The Empty House* twenty-three years earlier. It is not unreasonable to suggest that the poor quality of this story (and others) is down to Conan Doyle's decreasing lack of interest.

One final point regarding this story concerns the effects of Douglas Maberley. The arrival of his remaining property from Italy is the trigger for the visit by the land agent. It is odd that they were not intercepted en route to the Three Gables in order that they could be searched for Douglas's manuscript. Isadora Klein's claim that she wished to do everything within the law could be taken at face value but it seems unlikely in the extreme, bearing in mind what was at stake, that she would not have made an attempt to get the manuscript before it entered the house.

The Adventure of the Blanched Soldier

Published: November 1926
Set in: 1903
Client: James Dodd

Synopsis: Mr Dodd approaches Holmes to help him find out what has happened to his friend Godfrey Emsworth with whom he served in the army. Emsworth has vanished off the face of the earth since being wounded and Dodd has met with evasion from Emsworth's family.

Notes: This is the first story told by Holmes himself. After experimenting with telling his stories in the third-person with *His Last Bow* and *The Mazarin Stone,* Conan Doyle now used Holmes instead of Watson to tell the story. You would think that scholars would be happy with this after the third-person perspective stories but they are not. Dakin actually goes so far as to suggest that this is a fake case. However this is not to say that he is suggesting it is not by Conan Doyle. True to the spirit of 'playing the game' he infers that it is a fake because its inaccuracies render it so. His argument essentially is that Holmes would never pen an inaccurate account of a case as it would go against his golden rule that things should be seen as they are (or were). It would also make him a hypocrite of immense proportions if he were to turn in an inaccurate or romanticised account of a case after chiding Watson about the quality of his own efforts. So, based on all this, Dakin's position seems reasonable.

Once again, we have to return to the fact that the errors are Conan Doyle's and are consistent with the many inaccuracies he has been guilty of throughout the series. We must also not lose sight of the letter of 1908, to which we have twice referred, in which Conan Doyle made plain that he knew the stories he was writing were inferior to his earlier efforts.

The principal problem with this story concerns Holmes's recollection of the earlier adventure entitled *The Priory School*. Readers familiar with the story will know that it featured the Duke of Holderness as Holmes's client and, according to most chronologies, took place in 1901 a full two years before this story. In *The Blanched Soldier* Holmes refers to the case as an active one in which he is still very much involved but the school is now referred to as the Abbey School and the Duke as the Duke of Greyminster. Consequently we must ask ourselves is this the same case or a different one?

Blakeney suggests that they are the same case but that legal proceedings had continued to drag on in the two years since the case had been originally investigated. So Holmes's reference to 'clearing up' the case may have referred to his possible involvement in the trial or other connected legal proceedings.

This theory is good and it also explains away the potential inconsistency with Watson's living arrangements. At the time of *The Priory School* Watson was still living with Holmes yet in *The Blanched Soldier* Holmes states early on that Watson has left him for a wife. If the former case had dragged on for two years it is perfectly feasible for Watson to have moved out after the main investigation and for Holmes to later refer to the same case as a current one in which he was still involved (albeit without Watson).

The only alternative to Blakeney's theory is to conclude that the case was a different one that just happened to have a very similar title. However, this is so unlikely as to not be worthy of further investigation. So once again we are left with a slip of the pen by Conan Doyle that really should have been spotted before publication.

We can now turn to the other significant statement in this story. Who is this new wife that Watson had abandoned Holmes for? Blakeney informs us of a theory, put forward by a S. C. Roberts, which states that it could have been Violet de Merville from *The Illustrious Client* and this would fit given the story being placed in 1902. However it is not likely. Watson was living in his own rooms at the commencement of *The Illustrious Client* and had not yet encountered Miss de Merville. His only previous reason for living apart from Holmes was his marriage to Mary Morstan. If you accept the same reasoning on this occasion, he must have already been married and therefore his wife could not be Miss de Merville.

One of the many other objections to this theory, which Blakeney puts forward, is that the daughter of a famous general would be unlikely to marry a retired army doctor who was much older than her and, by the attitudes of the time, socially inferior.

Unfortunately we have little else to go on. Blakeney, Baring-Gould and Dakin all fail to offer us any other possibilities. It would seem that the latest Mrs Watson is destined to remain anonymous.

The Adventure of the Lion's Mane

Published: December 1926
Set in: 1907
Client: None

Synopsis: Holmes and his neighbour Harold Stackhurst encounter the local school science master, Fitzroy McPherson, staggering dazed near the coast where he had gone to swim. He collapses in front of them but manages to scream 'the lion's mane' before dying. Upon turning his body over they discover a number of whip-like marks on his back.

Notes: Once again Dakin is dismissive of this story on the grounds that it purports to be written by Holmes but is not, in his opinion, in his style. It is true that some parts are far removed from the style noted in the other stories but this is hardly reason to dismiss the story out of hand. You cannot help but wonder how many of the stories would be left if they were dismissed purely for changes in style.

The villain of the piece in this case is not a human being but a jellyfish. The Cyanea capillata or Deep Spiderfish is the largest known species of jellyfish. It prefers colder waters which would explain its presence on the Sussex cost. Its tentacles, which can reach up to one hundred feet, are the cause of the whip like marks that are found on McPherson's back. However, beyond the severe pain and redness that contact leads to, the results are rarely fatal. When principal suspect Ian Murdoch is also attacked by the jellyfish he survives and the suggestion is made by Harold Stackhurst that McPherson had a weak heart and this, combined with the attack, had led to his death. The other possibility would be an extreme allergic reaction similar to that suffered by some people when stung by a bee or wasp.

There is another inconsistency in this story concerning Holmes's reading habits. It is well known to most Holmes fans that Holmes and Watson had a conversation, in their earliest days together, where Holmes stated that it was his habit to only gather knowledge relevant to his career. In this story he admits to being an omnivorous reader with an ability to remember trivialities. It is this same ability that leads to him suspecting a non-human agency to be responsible for the whip-like wounds.

So how did Holmes come to know about the jellyfish? It is not going too far to say that the solution of the mystery hinges on the answer to this question. Clearly Conan Doyle had to have Holmes read about jellyfish at some point in the past. This means one of two things. Either Holmes had encountered a jellyfish before as part of a case, which is highly unlikely, or, contrary to what he told Watson, he made a regular habit of reading things that had no bearing on his work just in case they proved useful later. Regardless of which option you choose it is still a highly contrived way to end the case.

Returning to the issue of Holmes's writing style, Dakin's point about how it is different from the Holmes of the earlier stories is perfectly reasonable. In the opening paragraph, Holmes refers to the soothing life of nature '…for which I had so often yearned during the long years spent amid the gloom of London.' This remark is far removed from the Holmes who positively revelled in the gloom of London in *The Adventure of the Bruce-Partington Plans* stating, to Watson, 'See how the figures loom up, are dimly seen, and then blend once more into the cloudbank. The thief or the murderer could roam London on such a day…' It is clear that Holmes loved London purely because of the countless opportunities he knew it would provide for challenging his deductive powers. If you accept the chronology as detailed by Klinger, there are twelve years between that case and this one. Perhaps this could be long enough for a man's opinion to change but it is difficult to imagine such a change happening to Holmes. In *The Resident Patient* Watson says about Holmes that '…neither the country nor the sea presented the slightest attraction to him.' In view of this the Sussex coast would have been the least likely place for Holmes to retire to. A life of leisure in Sussex with a housekeeper and nothing more than beekeeping to amuse him would have surely driven him back to the cocaine bottle. Others have speculated that he spent his time working on his definitive work on the art of detection or began training with the secret service for his work in *His Last Bow*.

The Adventure of Shoscombe Old Place

Published: January 1927
Set in: 1902
Client: John Mason

Synopsis: Lady Beatrice Falder, who lives in Shoscombe Old Place, suddenly changes her habits after an alleged argument with her brother, Sir Robert Norberton, who trains and keeps horses on her estate. She is barely seen out of her room and her brother gives her dog away. Around the same time a moneylender called Samuel Brewer, to whom Sir Robert owes a considerable amount of money, disappears. Sir Robert's trainer, John Mason, calls in Holmes to investigate after one of his stable lads finds parts of a human skeleton in the estate's furnace.

Notes: The horse race is mentioned many times in this story as 'the derby' but what race is it likely to have been? Shoscombe exists and is close to Bath where there is a racecourse. A look at the calendar for 2008 reveals that there are two flat races during May which is given by Baring-Gould and Dakin as the likely month for the story. Assuming that the racing calendar has not changed too much over the past century it seems likely that Bath must have been the racecourse concerned.

   Current law in England and Wales states that a death must be registered within five days of it occurring. When Sir Robert explains his actions to Holmes he makes it clear that his sister had been dead for a week. Assuming the law was the same then as now he would have been in some trouble when the true facts came to light. However Watson tells us that the authorities were very understanding of the situation and Sir Robert received little more than a ticking off for his conduct. It seems incredible that it would turn out in such a way but at least it gives us a happy ending.

Dakin questions why the money lender Samuel Brewer would be prepared to lend money to Sir Robert after the latter had beaten him so mercilessly on Newmarket Heath. Clearly the money could have been loaned in advance of the beating and Dakin acknowledges this. However, the question of whether he loaned the money before or after the beating is not necessarily important. Brewer had a business to run and would probably want to maximise his chances of a return. Destroying Sir Robert in advance of the race, by calling the debt in, may have given him personal satisfaction but would not have netted him any money as Sir Robert had already placed all he could raise on the race. He could not have laid any claim on the estate as it was not Sir Robert's property. So, from Brewer's perspective, it was much better to wait until after the race and share either in Sir Robert's winnings or revel in his disgrace.

The Adventure of the Retired Colourman

Published: January 1927
Set in: 1899
Client: Josiah Amberley

Synopsis: Amberley comes to Holmes to ask him to trace his wife who he believes has left him taking with her a large quantity of money and securities. He believes her to have left with Dr Ray Ernest, his former friend and frequent chess partner.

Notes: As usual there is some disagreement about the date. Klinger places the events in 1899. Baring-Gould opts for one year earlier and, in this case, he looks to have the upper hand. Amberley's marriage to his young wife was over 'within two years.' According to Holmes's statement to Watson, Amberley married in early 1897 having retired the previous year. The question of course is exactly how far short of two years did the marriage come to its untimely end? This is clearly answered when Holmes despatches Watson to visit Amberley on his behalf and Watson states that his journey to Lewisham was on a 'summer afternoon'. This must be the summer of 1898 as the summer of 1899 would have been more than two years since the marriage.

This story introduces us to Barker, Holmes's 'hated rival upon the Surrey shore'. This is not a serious remark as Holmes later describes Barker as his 'friend and rival' and, towards the end, Holmes states that Barker has 'several good cases to his credit'. One is forgiven for being interested as to what these cases might have been. However, Barker suffers from the same problem as all characters that could conceivably be seen as equals to Holmes, namely that of rare appearances. However there is one thing that makes Barker different. With Moriarty, Inspector Baynes and Mycroft Holmes we are given very clear examples of their intelligence and abilities, with Barker we are not. All we know about Barker is that he had Amberley's house under observation and he later caught Holmes leaving the property. When Holmes later describes events to Watson and Inspector MacKinnon he states that Barker did nothing 'save what I told him'. If Barker was such a competent rival it seems strange that either he had no plan of his own or was prepared to shelve it and happily fall in with Holmes's intended course of action.

Once again Holmes gives away the credit of the case to the official police. As with Inspector Lestrade you have to wonder how Inspector MacKinnon would have taken to the true account of events being published after he had publicly taken the credit. However with a thirty year gap between the events and their publication the chances are that MacKinnon would have been retired for at least some years by the time the truth emerged.

Dakin is dismissive of this story and only offers an opinion on its possible dating because he tentatively accepts that it could be based on an actual case. In the end he comes down on the side of Baring-Gould and places it in 1898. Despite this he is very much of the opinion that this is almost certainly a fabricated story. Klinger, in his introduction to this story, disagrees strongly with this suggestion and the present author very much agrees with him.

Returning to the story, it is easy to view Amberley as an evil murderer but it is tempting to speculate as to how justified his fears over his wife actually were. Holmes makes it quite clear that he is unattractive by referring to his lack of 'outward graces'. Yet he was able to win the affections of a woman twenty years younger. Is it not possible that she was a gold-digger intent on getting her hands on the money he had made from his art supply business? Is it not also possible that she and Dr Ernest were involved prior to encountering Amberley and it was their plan to get access to his money via a sham marriage? If you extend this theory you could further argue that he overheard the two of them planning the theft and murdered them to prevent it. Certainly murder was an extreme reaction but not necessarily an unprovoked one.

The Adventure of the Veiled Lodger

Published: February 1927
Set in: 1896
Client: Mrs Ronder

Synopsis: Mrs Merrilow, the landlady for a Mrs Ronder, visits Holmes to request that he pay the latter a visit. Mrs Ronder is in poor health and has something on her mind which she only wishes to tell to Holmes.

Notes: The date of 1896 is not in dispute which means we can turn our attention to other areas. Watson states that a note from Holmes summoned him to Baker Street. The clear implication is that he was not in residence there at the time of the events he is describing. This is further backed up at the very end by his remark that he visited Holmes two days after the visit to Mrs Ronder and was shown the poison with which she had intended to take her life.

However Watson had moved back in with Holmes only two years earlier during the events of *The Norwood Builder* so why was he no longer at 221b? Some commentators contend that Watson had again married but this is swiftly dispelled if you take a look at the generally accepted chronology. *The Missing Three-Quarter* and *The Abbey Grange* are both stories in which Watson was resident in Baker Street and they are both, according to Dakin, set in 1897. Therefore the mythical marriage was a very short one. Klinger places *The Missing Three-Quarter* in 1896, the same year as this story, which makes the marriage even less likely.

Dakin proposes the very sensible solution that Watson was covering for a fellow doctor who was on holiday and was living above the surgery for the duration of the cover. Given the number of occasions that Watson had got neighbours to stand in for him (*The Stockbroker's Clerk* for example) this seems a reasonable theory.

At the beginning of the story Holmes informs Watson that Mrs Merrilow has no objection to tobacco so he is at liberty to indulge in his 'filthy habits'. Is this humour or hypocrisy? Given that Holmes was probably a heavier smoker than Watson (not forgetting his use of the needle) we must hope it was the former. You could theorise that Mrs Merrilow had made some disparaging remark about smoking in advance of Watson's arrival and Holmes decided to make her suffer although this would be a little unkind.

At the end of the story Holmes instructs Mrs Ronder that she is not take her own life as it is not hers to take. Some have taken this as evidence of Holmes's religious beliefs. His remarks to John Turner in *The Boscombe Valley Mystery* about answering for his deed at a 'higher court' tend to bear this out. However he also makes a remark that goes against this. When Mrs Ronder finishes her story Holmes remarks 'The ways of fate are indeed hard to understand. If there is not some compensation hereafter, then the world is a cruel jest.' If he were such a religious (presumably Christian) man he would surely have no doubt about the afterlife and its compensations.

Part Two – Holmes on the screen

The Best and Worst Screen Portrayals

Sherlock Holmes has been portrayed on film more often than any other character but when did he first appear? The first Sherlock Holmes film was entitled *Sherlock Holmes Baffled* and was a thirty second silent American production made in 1900. The problem for Holmes fans was that silent films did no justice to a character who relies on long passages of dialogue in order to reveal his deductions. When the industry gave birth to talking films the medium was finally ready for Holmes. It was a shame therefore that the first talking Sherlock Holmes film, *The Return of Sherlock Holmes* (1929), was such a non-Sherlockian event. The film starred Clive Brook and Henry Reeves Smith. It was not based on an existing story but did incorporate elements of Conan Doyle's work. Reviewers were quite impressed with Brook's Holmes but Smith's Watson came in for almost universal criticism. It is reasonably safe to say that Smith began the trend for overtly stupid Watsons. It was a blessing that he did not repeat the role.

The problem with the Sherlock Holmes stories is that very few of them provide enough material to be suitable for the transformation into feature films. This is no doubt why the film industry has often changed existing stories or created new ones with which to entertain us. Of those that are suitable for the big screen, the most often filmed is *The Hound of the Baskervilles* with over twenty separate adaptations since 1914.

If you look at the pantheon of actors who have taken on this challenging and sometimes damaging role they fall into two main categories which are, predictably, 'good' and 'bad'. These categories can be further broken down into 'remembered' and 'forgotten'. To the dismay of many an ardent fan, there are certain actors who fall into both the 'good' and 'forgotten' categories. When we say forgotten we mean that mainstream audiences simply are not aware of their performances. These unfortunate actors are largely only remembered by Sherlockian societies. Despite their notable contributions to the film life of Holmes they are destined to be permanently overshadowed by those who have captured the admiration of the wider public.

Here we shall list some actors who were notable and examine some of the films in which they appeared. The dates represent the actor's time in the role. For a more in-depth view at Holmes's screen career the best book to read is *Starring Sherlock Holmes* by David Stuart Davies (see bibliography).

Arthur Wontner

(1931 – 1937)

Wontner had been acting in films since the First World War and was generally cast in upper class roles as members of the aristocracy or army officers. His first film as Holmes was *The Sleeping Cardinal* (1931) which was a blend of *The Final Problem* and *The Empty House* along with some original material. He certainly had the appearance of Holmes but, at the age of fifty-six, he was arguably too old for the role when he first appeared. Nevertheless his arrival was greeted with delight by most fans of the time and his performances were well received by critics even if the films were not. His Watson was played by Ian Fleming (no relation to the author of the James Bond novels) in all his films except *The Sign of Four* (1932) where the role was taken by Ian Hunter. The films were set in contemporary times rather than the late nineteenth century (an idea that was to be used by other productions).

Wontner was cast largely on the strength of his performance in a 1930 stage production of *Sexton Blake*. Blake, also a fictional private detective, first appeared in the story *The Missing Millionaire* in 1893. He was very much based on Holmes and was even described as '...the poor man's Sherlock Holmes.' As an aside it is amusing to note that the first Sexton Blake story came out in the very same month as *The Final Problem*. Readers essentially were able to exchange one detective for another although Blake never enjoyed the same level of popularity.

The Sleeping Cardinal (which was known in America as *Sherlock Holmes's Fatal Hour*) opens with the murder of a bank night-watchman. Despite this and the fact that someone clearly broke into the bank's vault, no money appears to have been taken. Meanwhile Ronald Adair, a promising member of the Foreign Office, is lured to a secret location supposedly to meet a German diplomat. He instead finds himself in a room that contains very little apart from a painting depicting a sleeping cardinal. A man's voice coming from the painting informs Adair that he knows about his cheating at cards and will expose him if he does not use his diplomatic immunity to transport an illegal cargo from Britain to France. Adair eventually agrees and is told that he will be provided with a special bag for the purpose.

Meanwhile, at Baker Street, Watson is lured out of the way by a convenient medical emergency so that Moriarty is able to visit Holmes. The discussion between them is lifted from *The Final Problem* and ends with mutual assurances of destruction. Adair eventually decides that he will not help with the illegal transportation and is later found dead. Holmes deduces that someone shot him through the window of his room to ensure that he did not speak about the plans that had been described to him earlier.

The changes from the original story are strikingly evident. Adair is depicted as a card cheat whereas in *The Empty House* he is the man who discovers a cheat and pays for that discovery with his life. Moriarty, in the guise of Colonel Henslowe, shoots Adair whereas it should have been Colonel Moran who pulled the trigger (as Moriarty was dead).

Wontner's second outing as Holmes was *The Missing Rembrandt* (1932) which was known in America as *Sherlock Holmes and the Missing Rembrandt*. It was based on the original story *Charles Augustus Milverton*. According to *Starring Sherlock Holmes* by David Stuart Davies, Wontner provided a lot of his own lines for the film in order to make it more in keeping with Conan Doyle's dialogue. This did not save the film; the critics were not fond of it and rated it inferior to his first outing. Sadly this film is now lost so we are entirely dependent on the reviews of the time and are unable to form our own opinions.

Wontner's next outing as Holmes was *The Sign of Four* (1932) this time with Ian Hunter as Watson. The scriptwriter had decided to portray the romance between Watson and Mary Morstan and presumably it was decided that Ian Fleming was not suitable for a romantic role, perhaps on age grounds. Regardless of the motive it was decidedly unfair on Fleming but he was destined to have the last laugh as Hunter was not used in any of Wontner's other Holmes films.

The casting of Hunter presents the fan with a dilemma. He was well cast from an age perspective being the age of Watson as depicted in the original story. He was also believable as a romantic interest for Mary Morstan but his age was also the biggest thing against him. In the original stories Holmes and Watson are essentially the same age with at most two years difference. This has generally been reflected in the films that have been made with the actors playing Holmes and Watson being of similar ages – even if those ages have been wrong. Here we had a Watson who was at least twenty years younger than Holmes and it showed with Holmes coming across as a father figure showing his son how to solve crimes. Casting decisions aside, this version of the story stands alone as the only one to truly depict the full development of the relationship between Watson and Mary.

The film stuck to the central theme of the story but, as with other versions, introduced little changes, both necessary and unnecessary, which were, to a certain extent, forced by the contemporary time in which the film was set. An example can be seen with Mary Morstan. In the film she is depicted as a West End Florist rather than a governess. It was a small change but necessary as the concept of a governess had largely died out just before the First World War and was hence out of place in the 1930s. There were other little changes, which did not impact on the flow of the story, such as Mary receiving all the pearls from the Agra treasure at once rather than at yearly intervals.

The final scene in the warehouse by the Thames was decidedly inconsistent. The rather laid back and physically slow Holmes of the previous films was replaced by a boxing master. Holmes and Watson, having cornered the villains, take part in a very vigorous fight in an effort to overpower them and rescue Mary. This inconsistency was recognised by the critics and the film received varied reviews upon its release. Despite this Wontner continued to receive little but praise for his portrayal of Holmes.

Three years after *The Sign of Four* Wontner appeared in *The Triumph of Sherlock Holmes* (1935). The film begins with Holmes moving out of Baker Street to retire to the country with Watson taking over the premises as a surgery. Moriarty comes to visit him just before he leaves and they essentially repeat the discussion sequence from *The Final Problem* that they had already used in *The Sleeping Cardinal*. A few days later Watson visits Holmes at his new home and delivers a letter that had arrived after Holmes's departure. It turns out to be from an agent of Moriarty informing Holmes of a murder that is set to take place at a castle nearby. Inspector Lestrade then arrives to inform Holmes of just such a murder.

The story was based on *The Valley of Fear* and was pretty faithful but one of the most interesting aspects concerned Mrs Hudson. In the film we find her serving Holmes in his new home. This was clearly a regurgitation of the idea that Mrs Hudson followed Holmes into retirement to become his servant. The whole idea is absurd as Mrs Hudson, a lady who owned an expensive London property, was hardly likely to give it all up to become a domestic servant. Ian Fleming returned as Watson and continued to portray him as slow-witted, easily swayed by events and sometimes dismissive of Holmes's theories.

The final Holmes film in which Wontner appeared was *Silver Blaze* (1937) which was released in America under the title of *Murder at the Baskervilles*. Renaming the film for the American market had a very specific purpose. Despite the film being made in 1937 (and shown promptly in the United Kingdom) it was not shown in America until 1941. Basil Rathbone's version of *The Hound of the Baskervilles* had been out since 1939 and had been such a success that Wontner's final Holmes film was renamed to cash in on the publicity.

Set twenty years after the events of *The Hound of the Baskervilles* it begins with Sir Henry Baskerville inviting Holmes and Watson to visit him for a holiday. They decide to accept and walk straight into a murder mystery. The explanation of how Holmes came to be back at Baker Street, having moved out in the previous film, is not provided. Sir Henry is depicted as about fifty years old whereas he should be no more than forty. He also is a widower with a grown-up daughter called Diana. She is engaged to Jack Trevor who is a promising man with a semi-secret gambling addiction. The character of Trevor is clearly based on Fitzroy Simpson from the original story but the name of Simpson is instead handed to one of the stable boys who look after Silver Blaze.

Straker's motive for disabling Silver Blaze is changed although it is not clear why. The expensive mistress of the original story is replaced by large gambling debts. These debts are uncovered by Professor Moriarty who uses them to blackmail Straker into injuring the horse. However the prospect of having a mistress revealed to his wife would surely have been just as persuasive.

The inclusion of Moriarty was a significant mistake. The Moriarty of the books would have been decidedly unlikely to involve himself in race fixing and it is pretty clear that the invention of a different criminal would have been a better and more plausible idea. Pursuing this route would also have got over the fact that Moriarty had fallen to his death in the previous film.

In another large departure from the original story, more than one attempt is made to damage Silver Blaze's chances of winning the race and the second attempt is actually successful. Colonel Moran, Morarty's right-hand man, shoots the jockey with an airgun during the race thus disqualifying the horse from winning. This is bizarrely presented as a semi-happy outcome as all those who had bet against the horse, including Jack Trevor, win their bets and clear their debts to their creditors.

We shall skip over most of the other inaccuracies apart from two small changes. Firstly that Inspector Gregory from the original story was replaced by Lestrade. Secondly that Sir Henry Baskerville had managed to totally lose his Canadian accent.

Wontner died in July 1960. He falls very much into the 'good but forgotten' category and it is a tragedy that very few people are aware of his films. This is largely down to the fact that they are simply not shown on television and are only available direct from retailers. He is also hampered by the fact that he was soon followed by the actor whose portrayal was largely considered definitive for the majority of the century.

Basil Rathbone
(1939 – 1946)

One of the best actors in the role of Holmes, Basil Rathbone is best known from his films of the thirties and forties. Rathbone certainly had the appearance of the Holmes of the original illustrations and his initial characterisation was close to that of the stories. His version of *The Hound of the Baskervilles* (1939) was well set and an excellent production apart from one or two departures from the story and the dubious casting of some of the roles. This was followed in the same year by *The Adventures of Sherlock Holmes* which was loosely based on William Gillette's stage play. These two films were made by Twentieth Century Fox and were set in the Victorian era. Soon after these films were released the Second World War broke out and Fox decided to make no more films. Universal Studios later obtained the rights and immediately moved to secure the services of Rathbone and his Watson – Nigel Bruce. They also took the controversial decision to move the setting to the forties. They got away with this largely because audiences had already seen a contemporary Holmes with Arthur Wontner.

Modernising the stories had the distinct advantage, as those involved in Wontner's productions had already found, that it was far easier to film the series in a contemporary setting as it saved having to build too many sets. In addition the studio probably felt that Second World War audiences needed a contemporary hero to boost morale. The films thus became a good versus evil analogy for the war itself and this was reinforced by having Holmes face the Nazis in such films as *The Voice of Terror* (1942). Rathbone was inevitably forced to change his portrayal of Holmes in these later films. Had he had not done so he would have seemed anachronistic. Unfortunately it meant that his performances in the Universal films failed to live up to the initial high standard that he had set with Twentieth Century Fox. He was further hampered by the scripts, which were often poor. They inevitably directed him away from the original character as he was forced to demonstrate mid twentieth century morals and attitudes rather than late nineteenth century ones.

A notable aspect of Holmes that is absent from the Rathbone films is his use of cocaine. At the end of *The Hound of the Baskervilles* Holmes asks Watson for his needle but there are no other references to his habit in this or the other films. The drug habit was clearly an issue for American audiences and, to a certain extent, their British counterparts. This one drug reference was not seen by British audiences until comparatively recently.

You cannot think of Rathbone as Holmes without Nigel Bruce as Watson. Bruce's portrayal of Watson is a source of much debate. Some considered his comic portrayal to be excellent and in some respects it was but having Watson as a fool detracted from the whole basis of the partnership. Holmes needed a companion of intelligence and this was precisely what the Watson of the stories was. To show him in any other way does a disservice to Conan Doyle and the original material. It is absolutely absurd to believe that Holmes and Watson could have been friends, let alone room mates, if Watson had been such a fool. The effects of Bruce's Watson were to be felt for many years afterwards as some actors continued to make Watson a fool and a blusterer.

A regular feature of the Rathbone films was the tendency for the plot to either be based on more than one of the original stories or not be based on Conan Doyle's work at all. An example of an entirely new story can be found in *The House of Fear* (1945). Even though the opening credits stated that it was based on Conan Doyle's story *The Five Orange Pips*, this film's only real nod to the original story was its use of orange pips as a warning of imminent death. The film is actually quite good, one of the best in the series, and the fact that the events took place largely in a mansion, without too many contemporary features, rendered it almost timeless and thus made it possible to overlook the fact that it was set in the 1940s. *The Woman in Green* (1945) is an example of an amalgamation in that it contained elements of *The Final Problem* and *The Empty House* along with some totally original aspects and characters.

Rathbone made fourteen films (the latter twelve with Universal) after which his contract expired. He had begun to resent the effect that the films were having on his career and how his other non-Holmes work was fading into obscurity. This frustration was reflected in his autobiography, *In and Out of Character*, where he covered his time as Holmes in only eleven pages. He refused to renew his contract and no further films were made. His Holmes adventures were little more than B-movies so it was natural for him to fear how they would affect his future on screen. His decision had a negative effect on his friendship with Nigel Bruce as Bruce's own career was damaged by Rathbone's decision to quit the role.

In view of the fact that Rathbone starred in fourteen adventures, significantly less than the number of stories by Conan Doyle, you would be forgiven for wondering why the studios felt the need to invent and merge stories. The political purpose of the films featuring the Nazis was obvious but the decision to move the films to the forties probably made filming some of the original stories difficult as some aspects would not have translated well from the nineteenth century to the twentieth. By way of an example you need only to look at the issue of communication in the late nineteenth century. Despite the invention of the telephone in 1876 it was not widespread and telegrams remained a popular and common form of communication. They were also a relatively slow method of communication in comparison as the message had to be transmitted, translated at the destination and then delivered by hand on paper to the recipient. The recipient then had to repeat the process to convey a response. In some of the stories Holmes refuses, or is unable, to act until he has answers to telegrams he has sent. This allows the villains extra time to elude the authorities or progress their plans. For example in *The Adventure of the Dancing Men* Holmes sends a telegram to America with a question about a suspect. The answer takes two days to arrive which has the unforeseen effect of allowing Holmes's client to be killed before the perpetrator can be captured. In the forties the telephone was a firmly established tool and such delays were already effectively a thing of the past. As such a 1940s version of the story would not have worked without substantial changes.

Basil Rathbone died of a heart attack in 1967 aged 75 and is buried just outside New York.

Ronald Howard

(1953 – 1954)

The Adventures of Sherlock Holmes was a thirty-nine part series produced by Sheldon Reynolds and starred Ronald Howard as the Great Detective. H. Marion Crawford was his Dr Watson and Archie Duncan was a regular as Inspector Lestrade. The series was a conscious attempt to portray the adventures of the younger Holmes rather than the middle aged versions that audiences had become more accustomed to seeing.

Having made a good start on this front with Howard the casting went awry with Crawford. Crawford looked a lot older than Howard and his performance as Watson was too close to that of Nigel Bruce. This was only the first of the problems facing the series. The episodes were only thirty minutes in length which was too short a time to present a fully developed and self-contained story. The effort spent making the stories fit the running time had the unfortunate side-effect of making the series appear rather rushed. This accurately reflected the pace of the shooting itself. According to Howard, the episodes were produced at the rate of one every four days.

The finished episodes tended to have a long preamble and a hurried finish and consequently they seemed like books where most of the answers were on the last page. Howard's portrayal of Holmes was also a problem. He did not properly capture the appearance of Holmes and looked more like a Victorian dandy than a private detective. In addition he was far too excitable. In *The Case of Lady Beryl* his Holmes got positively animated and defensive when his chemical experiments were described by Lestrade as nonsense. Crawford's Watson, as discussed, was still far removed from the Watson of the books and was often reduced to the role of Holmes's hired thug.

Howard falls into the 'bad and forgotten' category. In some respects he was destined to fail. The short running time of the episodes meant that there was not a great deal of time for the story to develop or for the audience to attempt to work out the answer before it was hurriedly given to them. Additionally the series had come too close to the Rathbone era and Howard was lost in the shadow of Rathbone's Holmes.

After the series ended Howard's career continued largely in television roles and it safe to say the he fell far short of the fame attained by his father Leslie Howard. Crawford also spent a lot of his future career in television with the notable exception of the Fu Manchu films starring Christopher Lee. In these he starred as Dr Petrie who was very much a character in the Watson mould. In most of these films he starred alongside Douglas Wilmer who had, by that time, played Sherlock Holmes thirteen times himself.

Interestingly, Howard was born in Norwood in the same general area as that in which Conan Doyle lived and wrote many of the Sherlock Holmes stories. He died in December 1996.

Douglas Wilmer
(1964 – 1965)

Douglas Wilmer starred in the BBC series made in the 1960s. He was partnered by Nigel Stock as Watson. The series is highly regarded by many in Sherlockian circles and this is due in no small part to Wilmer who, to his credit, was a stickler for accuracy. The problem for the contemporary reviewer is that it is hard to get hold of any examples of Wilmer's work. With so many of his episodes apparently lost, Wilmer is destined, over time, to end up in the 'good but forgotten' category along with Arthur Wontner.

The first film he made was *The Speckled Band* (1964) which was one film in a series dedicated to different detectives. Its success led to the commissioning of a series of twelve further episodes aired in 1965. The stories filmed were *The Illustrious Client, The Devil's Foot, The Copper Beeches, The Red-Headed League, The Abbey Grange, The Six Napoleons, The Man with the Twisted Lip, The Beryl Coronet, The Bruce-Partington Plans, Charles Augustus Milverton, The Retired Colourman* and *The Disappearance of Lady Frances Carfax.*

The series had the look of the original illustrations (in many ways enhanced by being shot in black and white) and Wilmer in most respects had the correct appearance. Stock also went a long way towards making Watson less of a fool and closer to the man of action that he is in the stories. The problem with the series is that it does not really stand up to modern viewing. The surviving episodes suffer from truly awful incidental music and inconsistent writing. This was down to a less than competent scriptwriting team. According to Wilmer, he was forced to adjust or completely rewrite a number of the scripts, often at short notice, in order to bring them into line with the original stories.

According to *Starring Sherlock Holmes*, when the series was first shown it excited little interest. Based on the mediocre ratings the BBC lost interest and the series faded. When the series was later repeated it was put into a different slot and did much better. This prompted the BBC to consider a sequel. Wilmer's reasonable requests for improvements in production values were not agreed to so he bowed out and the BBC's hunt for a new Holmes began.

This was not the end of Wilmer's association with Holmes. He went on to record many audio adventures and is an honorary member of the Sherlock Holmes Society of London.

John Neville
(1965)

1965 and 1979 each saw a film in which Sherlock Holmes encountered Jack the Ripper. The first of these two films was *A Study in Terror* which starred John Neville as Holmes with Donald Houston as Dr Watson. It was not an original idea as W.S. Baring-Gould's fictional biography of Holmes had explored the idea of Holmes investigating the Ripper murders three years previously. Unusually, the film industry was to make a better job of bringing the idea to life, avoiding the bizarre theory put forward by Baring-Gould which we have already examined.

The film was nicely paced and used the idea that the aristocracy were behind the murders. However there was no suggestion that the Royal family were involved which made the film slightly different from most Ripper films that were to follow, regardless of whether or not they featured Holmes.

Neville made quite a convincing Holmes and Houston deserves credit for not playing Watson for laughs. He had his Bruce-like moments but otherwise turned in a good performance. It is a shame that some future actors, in their outings as Watson, could not have taken more inspiration from Houston's portrayal rather than from that of Nigel Bruce.

The supporting cast of the film was very impressive. Frank Finlay turned in a good performance as Inspector Lestrade and avoided becoming too much of a stooge. Robert Morley was an acceptable Mycroft Holmes in the physical sense but unfortunately he did not come across as the intellectual equal of Neville's Holmes. Anthony Quayle played the enigmatic Dr. Murray, the police surgeon whose secret knowledge went to the very heart of the mystery. There was even a brief part for

Barbara Windsor who audiences had seen make her *Carry On* debut the previous year. The film is still widely available from retailers and certainly is worth seeing but at the time it was not warmly received. The reviews of Neville's performance were ambivalent and it was very much the same for Houston. This was surprising as Adrian Conan Doyle expressed his personal admiration for Houston's portrayal.

Peter Cushing
(1968 plus 1959 & 1984)

Cushing picked up the BBC baton from Douglas Wilmer and the series continued with Nigel Stock staying on as Watson. The decision to retain Stock may have been driven by legal requirements. According to the *Baker Street Dozen* website, the series had to be presented as a linked sequel to the Wilmer series in order to retain the rights from the Conan Doyle estate. Stock's continued presence, whilst giving a sense of continuity, only served to highlight the change of lead actor. This is in no way a criticism of Stock's performance but, in the author's opinion, while a series can sometimes survive a change of Watson; it cannot survive a change of Holmes.

Cushing was not however the first choice to take over the role. John Neville, who portrayed Holmes three years previously, was approached first. This was presumably because the BBC wanted an actor more recently associated with Holmes in the public consciousness. However Neville refused and the role went to Cushing.

In his favour, Cushing was another stickler for accuracy and also kept the stories with him in order to preserve the integrity of the films. In addition he had the questionable advantage of having played Holmes before in the truly awful *Hound of the Baskervilles* of 1959. This was a Hammer Horror production and partnered Cushing with his long-time colleague Christopher Lee. Why Lee was cast as Henry Baskerville rather than Holmes is anyone's guess. Cushing was very much miss-cast on both occasions although this is not a universally held opinion. He did not have the classic Holmes look and, in his Hammer outing, he did not portray the logical side of Holmes as well as he might have done. This was not entirely his fault as the script was very much titled in favour of action scenes.

His performance in the BBC series was superior but offset by other factors that affected the production. Firstly, budget overruns meant that many actors who had been sought to appear such as Orson Welles and Peter Ustinov could no longer be afforded. This lack of funds was primarily down to the two-part adaptation of *The Hound of the Baskervilles* which went considerably over budget. Secondly, the quality was hampered by the infamous British weather which frequently caused delays in shooting. This had the effect that Cushing's version of *The Dancing Men* was actually broadcast before editing could be completed. These factors and the unexpected levels of violence led to the BBC being criticised.

Cushing's insistence on accuracy had one amusing result. In keeping with the stories and illustrations he always smoked a churchwarden pipe despite admitting that they made him feel extremely sick. In the year the series was released he was awarded the accolade of 'Pipe-man of the Year' by the Briar Pipe Trade Association.

Cushing reappeared as Holmes in the television film *The Masks of Death* (1984). Inevitably, given his age, he played an aging Holmes brought out of retirement for one last case. The cast was excellent and featured Sir John Mills as Watson but they were let down by a rather lacklustre plot. Like the original story, *His Last Bow,* the film took place on the eve of the First World War but instead of Holmes being a double-agent, doing his best to damage German pre-war preparations, he was involved in two parallel mysteries. The first concerned corpses being found in the Thames with horrified expressions, the second was the search for a missing German diplomat. It was not a great film and this has been reflected since in it rarely appearing on our screens or on the shelves of retailers.

Returning to the BBC series, it is a sad fact that the BBC was as careless with his Holmes outings as they were with Wilmer's. Of the original sixteen episodes a mere six survive. They are still widely available but it seems likely that Cushing, like Wilmer and Wontner, will ultimately end up in the 'forgotten' category of Holmes actors. He died of cancer aged 81 in 1994.

Robert Stephens
(1970)

Robert Stephens played Holmes in *The Private Life of Sherlock Holmes*. The film was set in 1887 which placed the events around the same time as those depicted in the canonical story *The Resident Patient*. The film opened with two men retrieving a box from the vault of Cox & Co. bank. This same box is referred to in the Conan Doyle story *The Problem of Thor Bridge* (published in 1922) from the *Casebook* series. A covering letter by Watson explains that the case described in the film is one that he had decided to write down and have suppressed until fifty years after his death. Hence the film is one large flashback.

The most impressive aspect of this film was that not only did it give us an interesting story it also tried to single-handedly tackle and explain many of the stereotypes and incorrect beliefs about Holmes and his world. One of the earliest and most amusing examples of this is where Watson and Holmes discuss the recent publication of the former's account of *The Red Headed League*. This leads Holmes to complain about how Watson's accounts have led to the public having an erroneous impression of him. By way of an example he complains that he has to wear the deerstalker hat purely because of Watson's accounts. He also blames Watson for the public perception of himself as a misogynist.

A mysterious invitation to see the Russian Ballet production of Swan Lake brings Holmes into contact with Madame Petrova. Backstage after the show she explains, via an interpreter, that she wishes Holmes to father a child with her. In payment she offers a Stradivarius violin. Holmes is only able to avoid this by making it clear that he has a homosexual relationship with Watson. The exchange where this comes out is very humorous and Stephens portrays Holmes's discomfort perfectly. Watson is, unsurprisingly, less amused upon finding out about the conversation.

This was a very clever idea in that not only was it humorous but it also tackled the single most erroneous belief that most people have about Holmes who are not familiar with the original stories. It drove home the point that this was something that Holmes said purely to avoid a difficult situation. This was reinforced by a later disclosure that he was engaged to marry the daughter of his violin teacher. Said marriage was only prevented from taking place by the lady's death a short while before the ceremony. Holmes's pain at this loss is supposed to explain his lack of interest in women since.

The main plot begins with the arrival of an amnesiac woman at Baker Street who eventually remembers enough to explain that she is looking for her husband who has disappeared. The search for this man takes Holmes and Watson to Inverness where they discover a plan to construct a submarine. The plan is being masterminded by Holmes's brother Mycroft on behalf of the British government. Christopher Lee was cast in this role and his Mycroft was decidedly antagonistic. It is clear in the film that the relationship between the brothers is often strained with Mycroft looking down on Holmes's choice of occupation. Colin Blakely played Watson as the intelligent man he should have been but he did also make him very excitable. His reaction to being effectively labelled homosexual by Holmes was an attempt to physically attack him. He also resorted to shouts of 'you cad' when he believed that Holmes has taken sexual advantage of his client.

Geneviève Page as Ilse von Hoffmanstal was clearly modelled on Irene Adler. This was reflected in the fact that she nearly managed to beat Holmes (an outcome only averted when

Mycroft explained who she was) and that when she ultimately died Holmes was affected enough that he resorted to cocaine with Watson's approval.

The original cut of the film was three hours long and had to be cut severely to bring it down to two hours. Inevitably, cutting a third of the film left the remainder looking decidedly disjointed and this caused the film to suffer at the hands of both critics and audiences. Stephens' Holmes came in for particular criticism. The principal charge was that he made his Holmes rather effeminate. The more often you watch the film the more marked this becomes. In many respects this was Holmes crossed with Oscar Wilde. As a result, although the overall film is adequate, Stephens' Holmes is destined to end up in the 'bad and forgotten' category.

Stephens died of cancer in 1995.

Christopher Plummer
(1977 & 1979)

Christopher Plummer was to star as Holmes twice. His first outing was a twenty-five minute television film of *Silver Blaze* released in 1977. Thorley Walters returned to the role of Watson that he had played two years previously in the comedy *The Adventures of Sherlock Holmes's Smarter Brother* (1975) and fifteen years before alongside Christopher Lee in 1962. Plummer delivered an excellent performance in which he stuck very close to the original text. However the short duration led to a rather rushed production despite the locations being excellent and the cast largely fitting. It is a shame that it did not lead to a series but Plummer was very much in demand and no doubt lacked the time to devote to such a series even if it had been proposed.

Murder by Decree (1979) saw Plummer don the deerstalker again with James Mason as Watson. This, the second Jack the Ripper based film, decided to trot out the Royal conspiracy theory. The film interestingly made the Ripper out to be two people with the whole purpose of the murders being to silence prostitutes who knew that the heir to the throne had married a Catholic. Plummer was inconsistent with his previous outing and made Holmes a man with feelings that were a little too evident at times. Despite the fact that he was clearly going against the known character of Holmes, he turned in a good performance. Mason was a non-bumbling Watson but was clearly too old for the role despite being entirely convincing as an old army campaigner.

The biggest problem with the film was that Holmes, Watson and all of the canonical characters were largely secondary. The main purpose of the film seemed to be to portray the Royal conspiracy theory that had first hit the headlines a few years previously. Holmes and Watson were simply used as a vehicle to carry the story and make it a film rather than a glorified documentary. In other words, rather than being a film about Holmes and Watson pursuing the Ripper it was more a film about the Ripper that featured Holmes and Watson.

The film saw the return of Frank Finlay as Inspector Lestrade and also of Anthony Quayle who this time played Commissioner Sir Charles Warren. This highlighted a tendency for certain actors to get cast regularly in Sherlock Holmes adaptations. Finlay was also to appear in the Granada Television version of *The Golden Pince-Nez* with Jeremy Brett.

Murder by Decree was not well received on its release and is, in many ways, an inferior film to Neville's *A Study in Terror*. More recent viewers, including the present author, are not inclined to be as harsh as the critics of the day.

216

Ian Richardson
(1983)

Ian Richardson starred as Sherlock Holmes in film adaptations of *The Sign of Four* and *The Hound of the Baskervilles*. They were released in 1983 and were intended to be part of a series of six films by American film-maker Sy Weintraub. Weintraub had spent a considerable amount of money to secure the rights from the Conan Doyle estate and was completely unaware that the copyright was about to expire in England. Weintraub had joined forces with English producer Otto Plaschkes to produce the films and they were filming their second, *The Hound of the Baskervilles*, when they heard that Granada was going to make its series with Jeremy Brett. A legal case ensued which ended in an out of court settlement. The settlement allowed Granada to continue and Weintraub stopped after the completion of the second film. In retrospect this was a good result as Richardson's outings were not without their faults.

The Sign of Four suffered the least tampering and is actually a good version of the story. However there were noticeable changes that were unnecessary even though they did not seriously affect the flow of the story. In the film Mary Morstan comes to Holmes after receiving a diamond, called the Great Mogul, by post. Conan Doyle's original story had Miss Morstan receive pearls every year for six years prior to her visit to Baker Street. The Great Mogul diamond was not an invention as it did feature in the story but it did not have the level of importance that it seemed to gain in the film.

The Scotland Yard inspector in the original story is Athelney Jones but, for reasons that are not clear, the new character of Inspector Leyton was created for Richardson's film. Thaddeus Sholto is killed in the film but there is no mention of this in the original text where the only members of the Sholto family to die are Major Sholto and Bartholomew Sholto. Thaddeus' death was clearly brought about in order to provide an action scene for the film but there was no obvious reason for changing the Inspector or substituting the Great Mogul for the original pearls of the story.

The final change from the original story came right at the end when Jonathan Small claimed to have thrown the Agra treasure into the Thames and Holmes demonstrated that he had hidden it in his wooden leg. This was clearly done to provide the traditional happy ending but in the book it was clear that the treasure really was thrown into the Thames. Admittedly there is no description of Small doing so but it is likely that he would have done in view of the strength of the bond between him and his friends and his desire to keep the treasure out of the hands of those who had not earned it.

Once again actor recycling was evident with the character of Major Sholto. Thorley Walters, better known for his turns as Watson alongside Christopher Lee and Christopher Plummer, took on the role of the avaricious Major.

Richardson's version of *The Hound of the Baskervilles* suffered from many more alterations. In the original story Sir Charles is lured out of his house, to his eventual death, in order to keep an appointment with Laura Lyons. This appointment is entirely innocent but in Richardson's film the meeting is moved to the conservatory where it is clear that they are meeting for a romantic dinner. The husband of Laura Lyons, who was only referred to by name in the story and most film versions, was actually made flesh in Richardson's film and was played by Brian Blessed. His sole role was to act the jealous drunken husband and be a suspect for the eventual murder of his wife. This murder, which does not feature in the original story, was carried out by Stapleton. The idea of Stapleton murdering directly was reused in the BBC's most recent version of the story. However it was not done in either the Rathbone or Brett versions.

The other problem with Richardson's *Hound* was Sir Henry Baskerville's lack of interest in the Baskerville estate. Sir Henry, played by Martin Shaw, stated that he had no interest in the ancestral home or the title and had only come over to settle the legal side before heading back to America. Clearly this overtly pro-American and anti-establishment Sir Henry was a nod to the republican sensibilities of American audiences.

The film continued the trend of using actors who had already featured in Holmes films or were destined to in the future. Nicholas Clay who played Stapleton was to reappear in the Granada series as Dr Trevelyan in *The Resident Patient*. David Langton, who played Sir Charles Baskerville, was to eventually appear as Sir James Damery in Granada's version of *The Illustrious Client*.

Richardson had different Watsons for each of his films and, regrettably, both fell far short of the ideal. David Healy in *The Sign of Four* (1983), did not portray Watson as a fool but he did act far too much like a love sick puppy. While it was perfectly in keeping with the story to have Watson fall for Mary, the image of the tongue-tied lover wearing his special cologne was a bit much. Despite this it would have been better if Healy's services had been retained for *The Hound of the Baskervilles*. His replacement, Donald Churchill, gave a very much inferior performance. According to *Starring Sherlock Holmes*, Richardson himself was not pleased with Churchill and stated his belief that this was largely because Churchill had little interest in the film and just saw it as the latest in a long line of roles. Churchill's Watson was also very contemptuous of Inspector Lestrade even though Lestrade was portrayed in a reasonable light and was clearly more intelligent than Watson.

The final word should be reserved for Richardson himself. His portrayal of Holmes was excellent in that he not only looked the part but had most of Holmes's traits captured perfectly. In some respects he showed too much humour especially on the occasions where he fooled Watson with a disguise but he undoubtedly gave us one of the best on-screen portrayals of the twentieth century. Repeated showings of his films should ensure that he remains in the 'good and remembered' category where he certainly deserves to be. He died suddenly in February 2007.

Jeremy Brett
(1984 – 1994)

For anyone born in the 1970s or 1980s the definitive Sherlock Holmes has to be Jeremy Brett. The present author would argue that Brett gave us the best Holmes to have graced the screen. However his first brush with the Great Detective was not as Holmes but as Watson.

This may come as a surprise to many and it is indeed rare for an actor to play both the side-kick and the sleuth. The only other example that springs to mind is David Suchet who played Chief Inspector Japp alongside Peter Ustinov before being cast as Hercule Poirot.

Brett played Watson opposite Charlton Heston's Holmes in *The Crucifer of Blood* at the Ahmanson Theatre in Los Angeles in 1980. The story, which was essentially an adaptation of *The Sign of Four,* was to be resurrected for the screen in 1991 with Heston reprising his role. Fortunately by this time Brett was established as Holmes in his own right and did not return to the role of Watson. In the author's opinion the casting of Heston as Holmes must go down in history as one of the worst casting decisions of all time. Therefore it is amusing that his one time Watson went on to give one of the best portrayals of the Great Detective.

Brett was an established but not hugely well known actor at the start of the series and this probably helped as it allowed people to see him as Holmes rather than as Jeremy Brett playing Holmes. In 1984 his first series as Holmes opened with *A Scandal in Bohemia* and it immediately became clear that it was a series that was going to do its utmost to remain true to the original texts. Brett truly inhabited the role and in the early episodes he positively shone managing to capture almost every aspect of the character as laid down in the stories.

The Adventures of Sherlock Holmes ran for two series with the second being shown in 1985. For both of these he was partnered with David Burke as Doctor Watson. Burke, whilst not always convincing in his role as a doctor, successfully portrayed the man of action that leaps out of the pages of the original stories.

The production values of the series were incredibly high and attention was paid to the smallest details. Gone were the cars and telephones of the Rathbone era. Horse drawn carriages and telegrams returned to their rightful places. The clothing was much more in keeping too. Not only were the clothes correct for the period they also kept very much in line with the Paget illustrations. The production was aided in this accuracy by Brett himself who, like others before him, carried the complete canon around with him and was not slow to correct dialogue he had be given if it deviated too far from the original text.

Unfortunately David Burke left the role of Watson after the filming of The Final Problem for personal reasons and also to return to theatre work. He made a personal recommendation to the producers that he be replaced by Edward Hardwicke. This was duly done and proved to be an inspired choice. Hardwicke's Watson was sometimes not so convincing as the man of action but his role as a doctor and man of learning he played to perfection. If merged together the two actors would have made the definitive Watson.

Hardwicke's first outing as Watson was in The Empty House, the first episode of The Return of Sherlock Holmes which aired in 1986. Again there were to be two series but this time they were separated by the first feature length outing.

This was The Sign of Four which aired in 1987. It still stands, in the author's opinion, as the best adaptation of this story with no significant deviations from the original text. This faithfulness paid off and the film was very well received by critics and audiences alike. The casting was first rate with John Thaw, who was rapidly making a mark as Inspector Morse, putting in an excellent performance as Jonathan Small and Jenny Seagrove making an admirable Mary Morstan. Of course, as with almost all adaptations of this story, the romantic interest of Watson and Mary was played down so as to avoid interfering with the partnership.

1988 saw the second series of *The Return* which included gems such as the excellent adaptation of *Silver Blaze*. In the same year Brett and Hardwicke gave us *The Hound of the Baskervilles*. It was extremely well cast but it did miss out one or two scenes from the original story which should have been left in place. Despite this the adaptation admirably resisted the all too common temptation, occasionally yielded to by others, of including a séance. This was the only downside to Rathbone's version and it is what makes Brett's version superior. Unfortunately the hound was less than impressive and critics were unkind about it and the film in general.

Brett and Hardwicke then took a break from the screen and enjoyed a successful run with the play *The Secret of Sherlock Holmes*. This was a two man show where the secret in question was that Moriarty was a figment of Holmes's imagination. The play ran for more than two hundred performances at the Wyndham's Theatre in London.

The series *The Casebook of Sherlock Holmes* began in 1991 with *The Problem of Thor Bridge,* which was another excellent adaptation, and continued with other good adaptations such *Shoscombe Old Place* and *The Illustrious Client*. Despite suffering from a much smaller budget than the early series it got favourable reviews which were welcome after the poor reception for *The Hound of the Baskervilles*. David Stuart Davies, in his book *Starring Sherlock Holmes,* tells us the both shocking and amusing fact that each time the cast needed to use the Baker Street set they had to pay extra as it had become part of the Granada Studio tour and was no longer under the control of the series producer.

In 1992, came the first of three more feature-length adaptations. The problem with these was that they were all based on short stories. In order the three films were *The Master Blackmailer* (1992), *The Last Vampyre* (1993) and *The Eligible Bachelor* (1993). The first of these, based on *Charles Augustus Milverton,* was a very good adaptation and kept the core of the original story very much intact. The casting of Robert Hardy in the title role was inspired and he gave a truly chilling performance. However to make it feature length a lot of padding in the form of original scenes had to be added. In this particular film the extra scenes worked well. Regrettably this success was to elude the producers for the next two films.

These films, based on *The Sussex Vampire* and *The Noble Bachelor* were terrible disappointments. There simply was not enough material in the stories to make the films. This led to both containing large amounts of original material which was in many cases totally out of place. The reviews for these films were inevitably less favourable than those that had been written for the earlier episodes in the series.

In 1994 the last series, entitled *The Memoirs of Sherlock Holmes*, aired. Alas Brett's performance was far short of his usual standard. He had put on significant weight and critics were quick to seize on this. However if these critics had done a little homework they may have been less harsh. Brett was by this time very ill and his extra weight was due to water retention which was a side-effect of his medication and nothing to do with diet. This ill health had a direct impact on the episode *The Mazarin Stone* where Brett only appeared in the opening and closing scenes. His place was taken by Charles Gray in his role as Mycroft Holmes.

Sadly the plans to complete the filming of the entire canon, which Brett had expressed the hope to achieve, were destined not be realised. Brett died from heart failure on September 12th 1995 at the age of 61. In the minds of many he will remain *the* Sherlock Holmes for the foreseeable future.

Matt Frewer

(2000 – 2002)

Frewer, generally known for his portrayal of Max Headroom, first appeared as Holmes in a version of *The Hound of the Baskervilles* released in 2000. More than one reviewer of the film was unimpressed with Frewer's take on Holmes. The principal problem was that he attempted to make his own mark on the character which was somewhat at odds with his remarks quoted on the *Baker Street Dozen* website.

'He has been played by so many actors in the past that the audience has certain expectations. After I've met these expectations, I can fill in the rest of the character.'

Audiences do indeed have expectations of the character and it can be quite confidently stated that Frewer did not meet them before adding his own touches. It has to be remembered that *The Hound of the Baskervilles* is a story in which Holmes features considerably less than the other stories. Frewer's performance suggested that he wanted to make the most of his time on screen and therefore he played up certain aspects of the character to the extent that all he gave us was an over excitable Holmes with a touch of Noel Coward and one of the worst attempts at an English accent ever committed to film. Physically however he was quite well cast being appropriately tall and a touch gaunt.

Leaving Frewer himself to one side, the rest of the casting and the screenplay were actually quite good. Kenneth Welsh as Watson gave us an intelligent man very much in the mould of David Burke and Edward Hardwicke. Robin Wilcock and Emma Campbell who played the Stapletons were very well cast each bringing the necessary attributes to the role. The same can be said for the actors portraying the Barrymores. The only disappointments were Jason London and Gorden Masten as Sir Henry Baskerville and Doctor Mortimer. London was slightly too young for the role and came across as too naïve. Masten was too old as Mortimer and difficult to take seriously as the late Sir Charles' close friend.

The final word on this adaptation has to be reserved for the hound itself. Instead of the gigantic fearsome hound given to us in other adaptations we were given an angry and blind dog that looked as if it would be more at home sleeping by someone's fire. This hound also made an appearance during the day which had the effect of diluting its fearsomeness.

Frewer's next outing was *The Sign of Four* (2001). This film suffered from a little too much tampering. We had an original character in the person of poisons expert Professor Morgan, a French-Canadian Mary Morstan and a Scottish Athelney Jones. Perhaps taking its cue from Arthur Wontner's version, the final boat chase on the Thames was replaced with a confrontation at the docks (presumably to cut down on costs). Inexplicably Jonathan Small's wooden leg was replaced with a damaged real one and Tonga was no longer a pygmy but an Asian man with considerable acrobatic skills. Despite these changes, reviewers were impressed and rated the film much higher than its predecessor.

Frewer followed this film with *The Royal Scandal (2001)* which was an amalgamation of *A Scandal in Bohemia* and *The Bruce-Partington Plans*. Aside from the absurdity of trying to blend these two stories we had the heresy of Holmes being depicted as being distracted from the case by the charms of Irene Adler. However Frewer managed to give up most of his more absurd costumes and began to give us a Holmes far closer to Conan Doyle's original. This film is considered by many to be the best of his outings.

Finally, perhaps mercifully, we were given *The Case of the Whitechapel Vampire (2002)* which was not in any way based on the canon. The scriptwriter, freed from the shackles of Conan Doyle's material, let his imagination run riot and gave us much more of a gothic horror than a Holmes adventure. In addition Frewer was allowed to drift back to the standard of his earlier films with absurd costumes and overplayed language. The fact that it was not based on original material also showed up in the dialogue allocated to the other characters which, thanks to the lack of canonical influence, was often flawed and out of place.

To date, Frewer has not appeared in any more Holmes films. The present author very much hopes that he will finally come to rest in the 'bad and forgotten' category.

Richard Roxburgh
(2002)

The issue of the ages of Holmes and Watson is one that is often overlooked. Almost all the film and television adaptations have them as men in their early to mid forties. In fact, the Holmes and Watson of the initial stories are about ten years younger than this. One has to wonder at the reasons for this persistent ageing of the characters. Perhaps it is believed that audiences would struggle to accept that two men in their thirties could be so knowledgeable and adept at crime solving. To date, only two films have attempted to depict the principal characters as they should have been. *The Hound of the Baskervilles* (2002) starring Richard Roxburgh and Ian Hart was refreshing in that it went a long way in removing the stereotypical aspects of the stories. The lead actors appeared far closer to the correct ages and the deerstalker hat and curved pipe were nowhere to be seen. However these great advances were offset by a catalogue of mistakes.

Roxburgh did not look like the Holmes of the illustrations which is vital in Holmes more than any other character. He lacked the thinness and his hair was the wrong colour. In addition his attempts at suppressing his natural Australian accent were effective but ended up giving him a voice that sounded like he was suffering from a sore throat. John Nettles' casting as Doctor Mortimer was a mistake as the Mortimer of the actual story is a man under thirty years old. Casting Nettles effectively increased the age of the character to the fifties. This miscasting of Mortimer had been repeated in versions of the story with Rathbone, Richardson and Frewer. Only Jeremy Brett's version got it right. The characters of Laura Lyons and her father Franklin were entirely absent. The omission of Laura

Lyons was a particular problem as it was a letter supposedly sent by her that drew Sir Charles Baskerville out to his doom at the beginning of the story. With her removed the role of female bait was passed to Beryl Stapleton who, totally against the original story, was murdered by Jack Stapleton. The séance held to communicate with Sir Charles Baskerville, which was dispensed with by Brett's version, was restored by the scriptwriter, Alan Cubitt. It was as bad an idea on this occasion as it was previously.

The final aspects of this particular adaptation that deserve criticism are the depiction of Holmes's drug use, which has been covered, and the positively hostile attitude of Watson towards Holmes. It is true that Watson was frequently irritated by not being kept in the picture by Holmes but never to the extent where he got openly hostile towards him. Watson's faith and trust in Holmes are apparent throughout the stories so it is a total nonsense to have Watson inform Holmes that he does not trust him at the end of the film.

On its release it was quite heavily criticised. Issue was predictably taken with the portrayals by Roxburgh and Hart and there was a certain amount of debate about why Richard E. Grant had been cast as Stapleton rather than Holmes. It seemed as if the BBC's awkward relationship with Sherlock Holmes was destined to continue.

Rupert Everett

(2004)

The initial poor reaction to *The Hound of the Baskervilles* prompted the BBC to postpone any ideas for further Holmes adventures. Some months later the film was repeated and gained much better viewing figures. The situation was almost identical to that which faced Douglas Wilmer's first series as Sherlock Holmes in 1965. As then the BBC was encouraged to change their minds and they commissioned another outing entitled *Sherlock Holmes and the Case of the Silk Stocking*.

Richard Roxburgh was not interested in reprising his role and Rupert Everett was cast in his place alongside Ian Hart as Dr Watson. Everett was well cast. He had the appearance of Holmes along with the manner and attitude. However this film, whose screenplay was also written by Alan Cubitt, continued the antagonistic relationship between Holmes and Watson that we had first seen in Cubitt's screenplay for *The Hound of the Baskervilles* two years earlier. The difference in this case was the change in the direction of hostility between the two men. In this story it was Holmes who was aggressive and dismissive of Watson despite the latter's best attempts to get him involved in the case.

The film was set in 1902 and explored the idea of a serial killer targeting the daughters of the nobility. It was a good idea but too many contemporary features were brought into the story. We had Watson's bride-to-be, in a role akin to a criminal profiler, advising Holmes on the kind of man he should be looking for. Although it is well known that America pioneered the field of criminal profiling, it was not a hugely developed science by 1902. In fact the forerunner of the FBI, the Bureau of Investigation, with its pioneering behavioural science unit, was not to be founded until 1908. Furthermore the concept of the serial killer was one that was largely unrecognised; in fact the term was allegedly first coined in the 1970s. Clearly multiple murderers existed but having Watson's fiancée speaking to Holmes as if it were a regular and understood phenomenon was absurd. She was also very irritating, constantly referring to Holmes as Sherlock. It is unclear whether Cubitt was poking fun at English stuffiness or American informality.

In the end the BBC's lack of fortune with Sherlock Holmes persisted. Critics were pretty much united in the opinion that the script was poor mostly thanks to the various anachronisms. Everett's Holmes was undoubtedly superior to Roxburgh's but not outstanding and it seems pretty clear that he will end up in the 'forgotten' category.

Jonathan Pryce
(2007)

Sherlock Holmes and the Baker Street Irregulars opens with the leader of the irregulars being chased by a mysterious lady with a gun through some London backstreets. He eventually leaps into the Thames in an attempt to elude her. Meanwhile Holmes, played by Pryce, is approached by Inspector Stirling regarding the death of two policemen who have been discovered with mysterious Chinese jade spoons. When the remaining irregulars come to Holmes for help in finding their missing leader he agrees to help in exchange for their help with the murder case.

Inspector Stirling later accuses Holmes of the murders when he discovers that both dead policemen had received the credit for cases actually solved by Holmes. This accusation is strengthened by the discovery of a box of jade spoons in Holmes's laboratory. Holmes avoids immediate arrest by calling in a favour from the Metropolitan Police Commissioner and is given seven days to produce the necessary evidence to clear his name and identify the true culprit. He is however forbidden to leave his room or receive visitors so he has to rely on the irregulars sneaking in and out of his room in order to receive information and issue instructions.

It transpires that the true master criminal behind the scheme is Irene Adler. She intends to steal a large quantity of gold and frame Holmes for murder. The motive for framing Holmes is apparently his rejection of her advances some time earlier. There are a couple of large problems with this premise. Firstly, the fact that Irene Adler is no criminal. In *A Scandal in Bohemia* she spent her time protecting the incriminating photograph of her and the King of Bohemia and eluding

Holmes. At no time did she attempt to extort money or commit any other crime. You could in fact argue that she was more sinned against that sinning. Secondly, she married during the course of the original story and therefore would not have pursued Holmes romantically. It is nonsense to portray her as the scorned woman out for vengeance.

The problems with the film do not end there. The casting of Pryce was a mistake despite the fact that critics seemed to like his Holmes. He gave us an absurdly emotional man who seemed prone to bouts of sudden despair. Bill Paterson, generally accepted to have been well cast, gave us a Watson who appeared very much in the mould of Burke and Hardwick but was let down by an apparent obsession with Battenberg cake. The Edwardian atmosphere of the film was damaged by a significant number of contemporary references which were no doubt included to engage the target audience. The language used amongst the irregulars was very much of today rather than the late nineteenth / early twentieth centuries and the film closed with the reunited irregulars walking down the street in the style of the film *Reservoir Dogs* with appropriate music.

Lastly, the film played around with the generally accepted chronology of the stories. It is made quite clear that Professor Moriarty and Charles Augustus Milverton are both alive and at large. Given the age of Pryce's Holmes, and therefore the late stage of his career he would have been in, they should both be long dead. None of these aspects affected the flow of the story and the film's intended audience were no doubt entertained. The errors and inconsistencies only cause issues for the dedicated fan.

The Future on Screen

The desire on the part of film makers to regularly alter the original stories for the screen is both bewildering and conceited. The clear suggestion from the industry is that the stories do not stand up well enough by themselves. Of course you can occasionally accept the argument that there is a need to generate new material to avoid accusations of unoriginality. There is also the occasional need to add extra material to pad out stories that would otherwise not have enough material to make a screenplay from. However the fact remains that the Sherlock Holmes canon has never been faithfully produced on screen in its entirety. As stated before, Jeremy Brett's series in the 1980s and 1990s was, in the author's opinion, the most faithful series ever produced but even it was not without fault. Many of the stories were not filmed at all and some of the later films were either padded out with new material or contained material from more than one story in order to make them run a suitable length.

Most fans share the desire to see the entire canon filmed faithfully but it seems unlikely that it will ever be done. Far too many elements have to fall into place and it is likely that that the task is beyond the will and wallet of most studios. The initial problem is that of casting. This firstly needs to address the issue of age. The men chosen to play Holmes and Watson need to fit the image created by Paget but also need to be in their late twenties to early thirties at the beginning of filming. If they were any older the project would be starting from a false position. In addition, at the risk of sounding controversial, the actors should be, wherever possible, the nationalities of the characters they play. Holmes and Watson should be English, Mrs Hudson should be Scottish and even one-off characters should be of the correct ethnic background. For instance the King of Bohemia should be German, Baron Gruner should be Austrian and so on. You might argue that you could cast anyone as Holmes providing he could achieve the accent and looked appropriate. However the counter argument is that portraying a nationality is more than just a convincing accent. Mannerisms and temperaments are as unique to countries as accents and you really need an actor who can capture and portray all these aspects. It goes without saying that an English actor has the best chance of capturing the character of an Englishman. Having said that, if you could find an actor who could achieve such a total characterisation people would applaud his casting regardless of his nationality.

The next issue is one of time. To film the entire canon would take some years and you would need to find actors prepared to commit to filming it. This would be difficult as most actors will do anything to avoid being typecast. You see time and time again in film and television that actors begin to resent the characters that made them famous. In many respects this resentment is similar to that exhibited by the authors. If an author or an actor becomes identified with one character and ends up playing second-fiddle to them you can see why they desire to shake them off. It was for precisely this reason that Conan Doyle initially killed Holmes in *The Final Problem.* However, such a significant commitment is necessary to film the entire Holmes canon.

The Granada series with Jeremy Brett managed to survive the departure of David Burke as Watson and the introduction of Edward Hardwicke as his replacement but the transition was far from seamless. Despite this the series recovered and soon it was possible to forget that the change had taken place. This was fortunate for Granada but we can be reasonably certain that it would not have been so successful had it happened with Holmes himself. As the pivotal figure in all the stories it is quite certain that the Granada series would have done significantly less well if Brett had hung up his pipe at any time. The disruption caused by a change of Holmes had already been illustrated by the change from Wilmer to Cushing in the 1960s BBC series. In an ideal world the principal characters of Holmes, Watson, Mycroft, Lestrade and Mrs Hudson would be played by the same actors throughout and any production that achieved this and stayed faithful to the books would stake a good claim to the title of 'definitive' portrayal. Fans of Hercule Poirot have no such worries as David Suchet has stated on more than one occasion his desire to film the entire Poirot canon. It seems that he does not fear being forever linked with one character and for this he is to be commended. The chances of finding an actor of the correct age who is similarly dedicated to the character of Holmes are slim.

The next issue is one of chronology. There is a tendency on the part of studios to film the most famous stories first. It is for this reason that the two most filmed Holmes stories are *The Hound of the Baskervilles* and *The Sign of Four*. It would be best if the stories were filmed in the order that they were written or at least very close to it. It is a well known fact that Conan Doyle did not write the stories in chronological order but as there is much debate about the true order of the cases it would be best to stick to the order of publication as there is no argument about that.

The final requirement is that the stories must be filmed in the context of the time. This means that contemporary morality and thinking should not be allowed to leave a mark. Attitudes should reflect the late nineteenth century and there should be minimal contemporary language. The current tendency to contemporise stories make this requirement unlikely to be fulfilled in the foreseeable future.

Bibliography

Baring-Gould, W.S. Sherlock Holmes - A biography of the world's first consulting detective. Published by Panther. ISBN 586-04260-1

Blakeney, T.S. Sherlock Holmes: Fact of Fiction? Published by Otto Penzler Books. ISBN 1-883402-10-7

Bunson, Matthew E. The Sherlock Holmes Enyclopaedia. Published by Pavillion. ISBN 1-85793-502-0

Dakin, D. Martin. A Sherlock Holmes Commentary. Published by David & Charles. ISBN 0-7153-5493-0

Davies, David Stuart. Starring Sherlock Holmes. Published by Titan Books. ISBN 1-84576-537-0

Doyle, Arthur Conan. The Penguin Complete Sherlock Holmes. Published by Penguin. ISBN 0-14-005694-7

Foley, Charles. Stashower, Daniel. Lellenberg Jon. Arthur Conan Doyle - A Life in Letters. Published by Harper Collins. ISBN 978-0-00-724759-2

Klinger. Leslie S. The New Annotated Sherlock Holmes Volumes 1 & 2. Published by Norton. ISBN 0-393-05916-2

Klinger. Leslie S. The New Annotated Sherlock Holmes Volumes 3. Published by Norton. ISBN 0-393-05800-X

O'Neill, Gilda. The Good Old Days - Poverty, Crime and Terror in Victorian London. Published by Penguin. ISBN 978-0-141-01938-3

Pointer, Michael. The Sherlock Holmes File. Published by David & Charles. ISBN 0-7153-7033-2

Pritchard, Linda. Warner, Mary Ann. The Jeremy Brett - Linda Pritchard Story. Published by Rupert Books. ISBN 0-9530-869-8-4

Rathbone, Basil. In and Out of Character. Published by Limelight Editions. ISBN 0-87910-119-9

Various Authors. The Further Adventures of Sherlock Holmes. Published by Penguin. ISBN 0-14-00.7907-6

Wagner, E.J. The Science of Sherlock Holmes. Published by Wiley. ISBN 978-0-470-12823-7

240

Also from MX Publishing

Portuguese Property Guide

"Contains a great deal of information of interest to potential buyers and people thinking of moving to Portugal"
Destination Algarve

"This book has a great deal of information for anyone looking to buy property in Portugal. It has been well researched to provide the latest information on living and working in the country"
Portugal Magazine

Seeing Spells Achieving

"For anyone with dyslexia, and any parent or someone involved in learning, education and health, these processes of visualisation integrate so well with existing teaching methods and they do give us all another tool, a new choice for growth and development to achieve new goals"

National Family Learning Network

Also from MX Publishing

The Gift – Real Life NLP

"It can be used in so many different ways from helping businesses to giving people the skills they need do better at school, while also being useful for treating phobias and helping people lose weight or stop smoking".

Daily Record

Performance Strategies for Musicians

"If you suffer from stage fright and performance anxiety then help is at hand"

The Pianist Magazine

Also from MX Publishing

Hurghada Property and Egypt's Red Sea Riviera Real Estate

From leading property writer Nick Pendrell comes a comprehensive overview of the Egyptian property market.

Succeed In Sport

Five times British Archery champion Jackie Wilkinson brings us the secrets to enhanced performance across all sports. Contributions from leading Olympians and leading athletes from Athletics, Running, Golf, Karate, Archery, Show Jumping, Cricket and more.

Also from MX Publishing

TOK258 – Morgan Winner at Le Mans

"I would recommend this book to anyone. It is the story of how skill and personal determination can beat the most elaborate, expensive and sophisticated machinery, the story of David versus Goliath. I warmly hope that it inspires the reader to try and achieve their own personal dreams" **Charles Morgan**

Enabled

Born with a disability that confines her to a wheelchair, this is the true story of one woman's dream and her pursuit of it against the odds. Engaging, heart wrenching and compelling are all words that have been used to describe this remarkable book.

Also from MX Publishing

The Beekeeper

From Canadian author Bernie Morgan comes the enchanting story of The Beekeeper. Originally in English the book is being translated into German and other languages as its appeal crosses the barriers of language and culture.

www.ingramcontent.com/pod-product-compliance
Lightning Source LLC
Chambersburg PA
CBHW071831020726
47502CB00004B/1310